THE CAPTAIN &
THE MERMAID

A Mystical Conquest

Laura Cyrena Kellogg

Dedicated to my Captain...

CONTENTS

I. WELCOME TO THE WONDROUS WORLD

of mermaids & mermen!

Fuchsia, the pink-haired mermaid, was a dazzling and majestic woman who was destined to be conquered by the bravest man in the sea. Glamorous and star-struck were those who crossed her path. No one could ever outshine her or dim her light. She was a wild creature who spent her days endlessly roaming without aim.

In a world full of mermaids and mermen, life was all about fantasy and fun. Days were spent hunting for food and feasting, while nights were spent drinking and partying. The merpeople were drunks who downed sea-cocktails like water. There was no work, only play.

The merpeople lived in the deepest and darkest part of the ocean, where no human could ever travel to. Their buildings and impressive architecture were leftovers from ancient human civilizations that had fallen and collapsed. They had gold, silver, and jewels from sunken ships. All their treasures and tools came straight from humans, due to natural disasters such as earthquakes and tsunamis, or deadly wars from human greed and violence.

Aside from the fancy buildings and lavish jewelry, their material world was fairly minimalistic. Hunters worked on spear designs and artists carved statues, but otherwise, physical items were few. They did not need technology, for their mystical powers were strong enough to go without it. Their tails allowed super-speed -- no need for technological transportation. Their eyes could see in the dark -- no need for lights. They were capable of sending out telepathic signals -- no need for cell phones or Wi-Fi.

The merpeople were unconcerned with technology, as their species witnessed many, many ancient human societies fall apart because their technological advancement ruined them. The most recent human world to fall apart was "Atlantis." Although this may have been eons ago, the merpeople had felt like it had only happened a few generations ago, for merpeople lived much, much longer lives than humans.

The Atlantis era led to technological advancement so far that the humans had absolute control of their lives, and there was no need for "God" or anything that was higher than them. There were no pregnancies: their babies were born in labs, designer-made and completely customizable. With enough money, you could have absolutely anything you ever dreamed of. There were no diseases or sicknesses -- at least not for the rich. And before death, they had the ability to preserve their consciousness inside of machines.

Also in Atlantis, the weather was completely under their control, so every day was bright and sunny. And there was no manual labor either, that's what the robots were for. The rich spent their days occupied inside of virtual realities. Even the poor lived decent lives, offered free education to keep up with society's extreme scientific progress.

Surely it seemed like the perfect fantasy, but with the advancement of technology came the inevitable decline of morality. People in Atlantis, so accustomed to getting their way all of the time, fought with one another like never before. Human interaction came to an absolute minimum as they much rather preferred to live life inside of computer land. People would only communicate with one another behind screens. And because of their refusal to get along and cooperate, wars were endless. It was a matter of time before they fought a war so bloody and brutal that there were essentially no survivors -- except the very few who had to start from the beginning.

This current world of human race was inching closer and closer towards destruction, just like every other era before them. Every single country, continent, race, and culture would perish all together as soon as technology would once again defeat the humans. And the merpeople would receive all their prior belongings, and all of history would be erased. The current humans were painfully oblivious of this endless cycle, thinking they have been the only ones to ever exist, that life simply began with the cavemen, that there hasn't been an infinite amount of worlds before them who made the same mistakes they were bound to repeat.

The apocalypse was an event that was always feared by the humans through each era of existence. As much as each country, culture, religion, race, and gender fought against one another, their true enemy was their collective worship of technology. That's what would be the death of them. So the merpeople stood back, preserving their mystical powers, and awaited human's inevitable fall.

The merpeople did not dare to involve themselves in the human world. They knew that their mystical powers would be exploited for money and power. It would be used as their new technology, and merpeople would be seen as soulless robots. The merpeople were strong and could put up a fight, but were far outnumbered, and wise enough to know that war was never the answer. Instead, they safely kept to themselves and lived in their own little world.

Now let's get back to Fuchsia, the leading lady.

Every week, Fuchsia would put on a show for her village. She was an actress and performer who loved to entertain and make others laugh. Her town would gather around a stage made of rock and cheer her on. Fuchsia reenacted famous stories such as classic fairy tales, putting herself in character and retelling the words with her own unique flair.

Merpeople were most fascinated by her hair. Just like her name "Fuchsia," the color of her hair was a deep red-purple-pink hue as vivid as the sunset. Her beachy waves flowed all the way down to her belly button. Wherever she went, they stared at her in absolute awe and told her how beautiful she was. She was a star and everyone was her fan.

Fuchsia had many potential suitors imagining themselves to be her husband someday. But she never took any of them seriously, knowing it was only lust. Her beauty always took center stage. Her *soul* was another story – something she found much more questionable.

Having just turned eighteen, Fuchsia began to ponder her fate. She believed marriage was in the cards for her -- but with *who*? There were countless mermen chasing after her...

There was Finn, who was a popular and macho man, very sporty and active. All of the mermaids always swooned over him. He was a huge flirt.

Fuchsia caught Finn's attention when her shows started gaining popularity. Finn noticed how receptive the crowd was of her, especially as she began her teenage years. He found himself to be jealous of her bewitching charm. The way the crowd cheered for her during the finales offered the validation he craved.

One night, after a show, he asked if he could join her on stage.

"In some ways," he persuaded her, "I'm an entertainer as well."

"Are you, now?" Fuchsia giggled.

"Yes," he urged, "I play tailball, and a crowd forms and cheers me on, because I always win."

'Tailball' was somewhat equivalent to a mix between American football and soccer. It involved a heavy ball made of gold. It was the most popular sport among mermaids and mermen.

Finn explained, "from the moment I was born, the second I popped out of my mother's tail, I got my hands on a ball and scored a point!"

Fuchsia chuckled in amusement, "that's a clever story -- for a moment there, you almost had me! So, you really *are* an actor, afterall!"

"I'm not lying!" Finn nearly screamed, face turning red, "it's true -- it really happened! You can ask my mom!"

"Is that what you wanna do -- play a game of tailball with me on stage? I'm an actress, not an athlete," Fuchsia rolled her eyes.

"No," he groaned, "write me into one of your plays, please!" And then he inched closer, "I can be your handsome knight in shining armor."

"Back off!" Fuchsia flashed her fang-shaped teeth at him, "it's a *one-woman show*. No guests allowed!" And from there, she stormed off.

But Finn, who could never accept defeat, from that day forward would do everything in his power to make her change his mind. Fuchsia, in return, was turned off by his stubbornness, and felt that he needed to humble himself a little more.

There was another merman chasing after Fuchsia -- his name was Reef, and he was a total mastermind. He seemed to play a lot of mindgames. Very sharp and clever, he was always one step ahead of the game.

Right as Fuchsia was about to get on stage for her show, Reef stopped her to quickly say, "good luck with your performance of 'Midnight Castle.'"

Wide-eyed, Fuchsia wondered, "how did you know I was going to reenact that story? It was supposed to be a surprise!"

"I know things," he grinned before scurrying away.

Perplexed, Fuchsia had an idea -- next week, before her show, she would loudly announce to her sisters that she'd be doing 'Three Blind Mice,' when truthfully, she'd be doing 'Country Mouse, City Mouse.'

"Can't wait for you ladies to see 'Three Blind Mice!'" Fuchsia called out to them, obnoxiously loud, before swimming to the stage.

But just then -- Reef caught her, and told her, "good luck with 'Country Mouse, City Mouse!'"

Jaw dropping, Fuchsia began, "how did you..."

Again, he smirked with, "I know things," and once again scurried away.

Fuchsia growled like an angry cat, frustrated with Reef's smugness. His know-it-all cockiness disgusted her.

"Hold on!" Fuchsia attempted to stop him, but Reef was already out of sight. So she chased after him for what felt like miles and miles until she finally caught up to him.

"Hmm?" Reef paused to let Fuchsia catch him.

"Reef, you don't know *everything*, okay!?" Fuchsia angrily pouted.

"I know about your feelings for me," Reef smiled, which set Fuchsia off like a pistol.

"I do *not* have feelings for you!" She threw her hands in the air.

Without a beat, Reef instantly responded, "then what are you doing, swimming after me, trying to pick a fight?" He raised an eyebrow, "looks to me like you've got a little crush."

"Oh, please!" Fuchsia rolled her eyes, "I just..." suddenly, she was speechless.

"You just...?" Reef leaned in, patiently waiting for her to continue.

"I just don't like how smug you are, is all."

"Then why are you still talking to me?"

"Whatever!" Fuchsia stuck out her tongue and swam away.

While swimming back, she couldn't help but think... *wait... why did I chase him down? Maybe I do have feelings for him? No, no! Of course not! ...Or do I!?*

Reef knew how to get inside of Fuchsia's head -- that was for sure. She constantly questioned whether she genuinely had feelings for him, or if he was succeeding at his mind games. Although, as much as Reef could claw himself inside of Fuchsia's head, she could never find his way inside of her heart.

There was Gill, who was sweet and shy. He seemed to be very sensitive, emotions running deep over his cool exterior. Gill had a sense of vulnerability that the other memen didn't have.

Fuchsia was putting on yet another show for her village, when she noticed a boy in the front row -- it was Gill -- shedding a tear. After her one-woman play was over, she ran up to Gill before he could escape the crowd. She couldn't let him get away.

"Excuse me," Fuchsia said, softly touching his shoulder, "I don't mean to embarrass you or anything -- but was that a tear I saw?"

"Oh, goodness!" Gill covered his face, bashfully, "I do get a little carried away when I watch your performances."

"You do?" Fuchsia's face lit up. She knew she could make her audience laugh -- but was astonished to see she could make someone cry. "Hopefully those were *good* tears," she added, "and I haven't done anything to upset or offend you!"

"Oh, no," he shook his head swiftly, "I was so moved by your story," he told her with a quiet voice, bowing his head down, unable to look her directly in the eyes. "That scene when the main character has to say goodbye to her parents forever -- it broke my heart."

Speechless, all Fuchsia could do was place her hand on her heart with sympathy.

"I'm so sorry," he apologized.

"Sorry!?" Fuchsia furrowed her eyebrows, "why in heavens would you ever be sorry? You made my day! In fact, you made my whole acting career!" She threw her hands into the air with cheer.

"I've got to go," he half-smiled, flustered.

Before Fuchsia could thank him for his kindness, he was already out of sight. From there forward, Gill would continue to appear at Fuchsia's shows -- but never again in the front row, where she could view the sparkle of his eyes. Instead, he would always sit coyly in the far back, where he could remain partially hidden. As much as Fuchsia was attracted to Gill's sensitivity, he was far too shy to ever pursue her completely.

Oceanus, another merman, was a huge clown and had a wild sense of humor. He always knew how to make Fuchsia laugh.

Sometimes, during shows, Oceanus would try to make himself a part of the play and scream jokes from the crowd. In which, Fuchsia would crack up, getting totally distracted from her script.

As Fuchsia was the only actress in her show, she would play multiple characters -- whether female or male. One time, there was a heavy love scene, in which she had to switch back and forth between the woman and the man.

"Kiss! Kiss! Kiss!" Oceanus chanted, and in return, the rest of the crowd -- including Fuchsia herself -- roared with laughter.

"This is a G-rated story!" Fuchsia defensively teased back.

Fuchsia adored how Oceanus always made her giggle, but being such a jokester, she questioned if he was capable of ever being serious with her.

And yet another merman, Archer, was a high achiever with strong determinism and ambition.

Quite often, Archer would greet Fuchsia right before her shows with a bouquet of lilies, or a collection of shells, and wish her luck. At one point, it all got to be too much, and Fuchsia was forced to turn him down.

"But I love to bring you gifts!" Archer pleaded, "it's my favorite thing to do!"

"It's just a little too much," Fuchsia sighed, pushing away his hand full of colorful stones.

"I see," Archer nodded before disappearing into the blue. Fuchsia felt awful, however, it had to be done.

Once her show was over that night, Archer appeared again.

"Come with me," he smiled.

"Alright..." Fuchsia skeptically followed him, knowing this was probably a mistake.

Screaming at the top of her lungs, Fuchsia tried to comprehend what she was looking at once they arrived to their destination -- a gigantic sea monster, bigger than any fish she had ever seen in her life!

"It's okay!" Archer assured, "it's dead!" He pointed out several arrows poking out of its side.

"What happened!?" Fuchsia shrieked.

"It's the biggest monster of the sea!" He exclaimed with pride, "I hunted him down just for you!"

"H-how!?" She stuttered, still in disbelief.

"Well," Archer described, "when you rejected me, it struck some type of nerve -- suddenly, I was overcome with a strength and power I have never known before. I had to do anything -- *anything* -- to impress you and win you back."

Fuchsia was flabbergasted.

"This anger and pain inside of me awoke a deep beast inside of me, a merciless creature hungry for your love," pointing again at the monster, he continued, "this here represents my love for you!"

"Archer!" Fuchsia yelled at him in fury, "I told you already -- no more gifts!"

"It's not a gift! It's an act of love."

"Archer, you *killed* this poor, innocent creature!" Fuchsia nearly began to cry, "that's not love! You should be ashamed of yourself!"

Displeased, Archer bowed his head, "I'm sorry -- I just wanted to impress you."

"Why don't you impress me by leaving me alone!?" Fuchsia groaned.

"Okay," Archer agreed -- almost too literally.

From that day forward, Archer would leave Fuchsia alone -- but she would always feel him lurking in the background, secretly watching her. From time to time, she stumbled upon random collections of lilies or rocks, and knew exactly where they came from.

Fuchsia was gracious for Archer's dedication to her, but it certainly crossed her personal boundaries.

Finn, Reef, Gill, Oceanus, and Archer would all compete for Fuchsia's love. However, as hard as they tried, none of them could compete with Marino.

Marino was a merman who Fuchsia had known since childhood. They had always been friends and nothing more, but everyone had the feeling that they would end up getting married someday. Fuchsia pondered if perhaps it was time to give him a chance. Out of all the mermen, he was the easiest for her to open up to. It was too difficult to describe Marino in a few sentences, he was multifaceted with many layers.

Marino was friendly and outgoing just like Finn, he was clever like Reef, he was sensitive like Gill, he was hilarious like Oceanus, and he was focused like Archer. Marino was the whole package. And yet, there was something missing. Fuchsia couldn't put her finger on it.

Her whole life, Fuchsia had been a fiercely independent mermaid and therefore never felt the need to have a boyfriend or potential husband. But since her coming of age, she could not stop thinking about love. She always thought of marriage as her *"someday,"* yet with the passing of time, this hypothetical concept was now becoming a reality.

In the merpeople world, marriage was taken very lightly. Mermaids and mermen married quickly and impulsively, typically as soon as they entered adulthood. And with the rush of marriage also came the rush of separation. Many couples were in open relationships, some even married in groups of three or four. There was no government involved, simply a consensual promise. It wasn't as structured as it is in the human world.

Fuchsia respected her culture's attitude towards marriage, but she craved something different. She wanted a love that was just like the old fairy tales she performed for her peers. She wanted a prince to rescue her and have eyes for only her. She desired one merman who would worship her like a royal goddess, and no one else -- for eternity.

Fuchsia's sisters laughed at her silly, little dream. They urged her not to be so arrogant and egotistical, expecting any merman to completely focus on her for the rest of his life. They told her it wasn't realistic, how mermaids and mermen are designed to *explore*, not to be tied down like an anchor.

But Fuchsia had grown so incredibly bored of her safe life. All of the fun and flirting, mermaids and mermen bouncing around between each other, felt so shallow. She craved a connection so deep that it would challenge her, that it would force her to go beyond her limits.

II. THE CAPTAIN'S CONQUEST

It was simply another day, when eighteen-year old Fuchsia felt the crushing sense of purposelessness weigh her down much heavier than usual. Thoughts of what the future held bombarded her like a school of fish. Is this what life would be like forever -- floating around, watching all the mermen take turns doing anything to catch her eye? Would it always be these little games? Would she continue to roll her eyes at all of them, or could one of them finally reach deep enough to pull on her heartstrings?

Putting on shows and making the crowd laugh had grown incredibly tiring. She was a temporary distraction to her audience -- an escape from boredom.

Living as a mermaid was an endless cycle of eat, sleep, party, and repeat. You hunt for fish, sleep soundly in your cave, scarf down sea-cocktails, and then do it all over again. It was the same predictability every day. There were no challenges to overcome, no mysteries to solve, no soul growth... Fuchsia thought, there had to be more to life than this. There must be such a thing as a whirlwind romance that can shake you to your core.

Desperate for an escape, Fuchsia decided to swim far towards the surface of the sea. It was dangerous, it was forbidden -- and it was exactly what Fuchsia craved.

Popping her head above water, it felt so peculiar to breathe in the fresh air. She propped herself up on a smooth rock where she could sit up straight and let her tail dangle freely in the water. The heat of the sun made her smile as rays of sunlight glimmered upon her skin.

All alone, she felt so free. Fuchsia was so accustomed to being constantly watched -- by her audience as she performed, by her adoring fans as she went about her day, or by her protective older sisters when she was at home just trying to relax. And now, finally: sweet isolation.

Fuchsia lifted her head to watch the birds fly by. They seemed like the freest creatures of them all. She lifted her arms like wings, splashed her tail around, and imagined herself flying amongst them.

"I'm a bird!" she cheered with joy.

Flying past her, the birds twittered, as she imagined they were replying back to her, "yes, you are!" as if they were cheering her on.

Fuchsia giggled at her silly imagination. Of course the birds were simply going with the wind, following their genetic code, completely unaware of any world outside of their own. But Fuchsia liked to imagine otherwise -- that they too, were her fans.

After the birds had passed, she was now completely alone. Nothing but the sea surrounded her. She couldn't see any land, nor trees or animals, from her little rock she was hoisted upon. How unusual, that this rock was sticking out in the middle of nowhere, as if someone had planted it on purpose, hoping a lonely soul would come and sit.

Although it was technically not a little rock, not underneath the surface. Below water it was a gigantic volcanic mountain, its tip sticking out ever so slightly above.

Totally stranded, not a single soul in sight, Fuchsia felt stillness like never before. It was far too quiet. And it made her uncomfortable. So she began to hum.

Hmm... hmm... hmm... she purred.

Her humming swiftly morphed into singing, and the next thing she knew, Fuchsia was belting her heart out.

How odd it was that no one was applauding or singing along. So she sang even louder, until her voice echoed across the ocean. Indeed, she was a bird -- and her voice was her wings.

Fuchsia closed her eyes and let herself soar. Never before had she felt such freedom. In that moment she realized she was more than an entertainer, she was pure expression. Could it be, she wondered, that external validation is more limiting than it is encouraging? Her voice had never sung this high and loud before!

Bursting her eyes wide upon, her heart sank when she spotted a blurry figure in the distance. So she did have an audience after all. It looked like some sort of unfamiliar beast. Until it came a bit closer... and... she gulped. She had seen one of these before. It was a ship. And with every ship, comes a human.

Zipping her lips as her singing came to a sudden halt, Fuchsia froze in absolute fear. The ship was headed her way now at full speed. And on this ship was not just any other human, but a captain, uniform and all!

Fuchsia had always been taught to avoid humans at all cost -- if you see one, swim away as fast as you can! She was told that the human world was the greatest threat to the survival of mer-people -- they were too greedy, occupied with money, and fixated on domination over the planet. If humans could prove the existence of mermaids and mermen, they would start a war and attempt to exploit them for wealth, power, and continued deterioration of the environment. They would never allow them to co-exist in peace.

But something inside of her told her to stay, overcome with tempted curiosity. Closer now, she could get a better look at this captain. He was actually quite dashing -- not like those rugged, dirty pirates. He also looked quite smitten -- even from a distance she could see that he was blushing. His prominent cheeks were pink like roses. The captain was staring at her intently with his binoculars.

Now fear was taking over. Fuchsia had been told many tales about human encounters. Some claim to have been captured by them, typically the pirates, but somehow managed to get away last minute. Some even claim they've been caught on camera, but were able to destroy the evidence.

And that's why they say, "never, ever, swim to the surface of the sea."

Woops.

But Fuchsia had also heard other, more exciting tales about human encounters. Some mermaids have gushed about how the sailors are a lot more handsome, and a lot more fun, than the mermen. They say that lonely sailors who have been stranded from civilization for an extended period of time, trapped in the middle of the ocean, will do anything to please a mermaid.

And with that thought, Fuchsia's fear turned back into bravery and friskiness. So Fuchsia slid off the rock and swam right up to the boat. It was the most treacherous thing she'd done in her life!

The man on the boat stood tall and proud with his chest pointing high towards the sky. It looked like he, too, was up for a challenge. He must be so bored and lonely, like me, Fuchsia thought.

The Captain was well aware of the danger of mermaids. He heard many myths about men who sail the sea and succumb to mermaid tricks. Seduced by their magical beauty, the mermaids lure them in and then eat them alive!

But that didn't stop the Captain. He was a confident man.

"Hello, beautiful!" he called out in mesmerization.

"Hello, handsome," she softly greeted.

Now he was close enough to see the color of her gorgeous eyes: a blue-green hue, like seafoam. And Fuchsia could see his heavenly hazelnut eyes.

There was such intense heat between the two of them, like neither of them had ever experienced before. Visions of fire burst through their heads.

"What a delightful voice you have!" he exclaimed. A full-grown man, he was looking at her like a giddy child. "Why did you stop singing? Please, keep going..." he nearly begged.

Fuchsia remained frozen as her thoughts ran mad. She was used to having males being putty in her hands, but surely never one this handsome. She examined him from head to toe: freshly trimmed hair, a bit of stubble on his face, rosy cheeks, and a towering posture, all wrapped up in a sailor's uniform. He was certainly older and far more distinguished than her, but maintained a youthful glow.

"What is it?" he asked, uncomfortable with her glaring silence. "What brings you out here, all alone? Don't you know it's not safe out here?" He looked around – no one else in sight – nothing but the sea.

"I've grown bored," Fuchsia sighed, "and yourself? Don't you know it's murderous to confront a mermaid? Haven't you heard the fables of captains who are eaten alive, because they came too close to a beautiful mermaid?" Emphasizing the threat of her species, Fuchsia felt powerful.

"Aha," he nodded with amusement, "luckily, I have the safety of my ship. You're the one treading alone in water," he pointed out. The Captain seemed more concerned for Fuchsia's protection than his own.

"Come join me for a swim," Fuchsia seductively suggested, running her fingers through her hot pink hair. Even she was surprised by her own forwardness.

The Captain raised an eyebrow...

Both the Captain and the Mermaid had much to lose. The Captain risked getting devoured by the Mermaid, while the Mermaid risked being caught by the Captain and possibly exposing the existence of mermaids to the entire world.

However, both the Captain and the Mermaid also had so much to gain. Here was their chance to both have an experience like never before. The Captain would get a taste of the forbidden mermaid world, while the Mermaid would get a taste of the forbidden human world.

"Don't you ever wonder..." Fuchsia began, speaking slowly with suspense, "what do the scales of a mermaid feel like? Can they grant wishes? Can you steal magic from this mermaid?"

"I better stay on my ship," he shook his head, "I've already gotten myself into enough trouble."

Aggravated by his hesitancy, Fuchsia concluded that she would have to try a bit harder to seduce the Captain.

"Please," she begged in her sultriest voice, "you look so warm and dry up there on your lonely ship. Cool down, take a swim..." She brushed her fingertips against the surface of the water, admiring the ocean, before looking back up at the Captain with wide eyes.

The Captain was sweating, and he knew it wasn't from the sun.

"Say no more!" The Captain, entranced, ripped off his shirt and splashed into the water.

Fuchsia was nearly disappointed with how easy it was to capture him, but her heart raced with excitement and adrenaline to be this close. And now they were merely inches away from one another, staring eye-to-eye with intent focus. She smiled at him with victory.

"Do you think I'm going to drown you?" Fuchsia teased.

He smirked at her with arrogance, "is that what you do to all the other sailors?"

"Oh," Fuchsia swiftly shook her head, "I would never let any other sailor get this close. If they did, I would surely eat them alive."

"Then why me?" He asked, "why have I been spared?"

"That's a question for the heavens."

"You should know that I'm not just any sailor, I am the Captain."

"Oh, is that right?"

"It sure is."

"This is your lucky day, Captain."

"What are you going to do with me?"

Fuchsia never imagined she would get this far. For, she had never come face to face with any human before. Entangling herself this much in the human world was insanity. And yet his energy was magnetic... and their chemistry was out of control...

Speechless, the two of them leaned into each other until they could no longer bear the gravity. They held each other for a moment before the Captain reached in for a kiss. The tip of his soft lips grazed hers ever so slightly.

And then, before their lips could firmly meet, Fuchsia pulled away as fear took over once again. It was as if there was some form of trust building between the two of them and it was unsettling for her. She wondered, "why isn't he trying to capture me? Is it all a part of his plan?"

"What is it?" The Captain asked, "did I disappoint you?"

"No!" Fuchsia shook her head, "I didn't expect to feel that way..."

"What way?"

"I have kissed many boys before..." Fuchsia thought out loud, "but you felt so different... is it because you're forbidden, is that why?"

"And I've kissed a lot of girls!" The Captain defended himself after getting hit with a sharp pang of jealousy.

"I feel so strange," she giggled, "is this normal? Do you feel it too?"

"I think you're the most beautiful woman I've ever laid eyes on."

"Oh, I know that," she shrugged with an eye roll, "but do you... feel something?"

"Yes," he nodded without hesitation, "I love you, I'm in love with you!"

Fuchsia burst into a fit laughter, "you love me? You don't even know me!"

The Captain let her finish laughing, paused for a moment, and then said in total seriousness, "once in a blue moon, two souls recognize each other from previous lifetimes with just one glance. There is this deep, inner, intuitive feeling that cannot be explained by ration or logic. You know that you've met the one. You just know it. This phenomenon is called 'love at first sight.' And I love you, even though I've just met you."

Fuchsia was astounded. Blown away. Frozen. Out of all the pickup lines she had heard before, this one was out of this world.

"Oh," was all she could say.

And that was responded with total disappointment upon the Captain's face.

"Wait, no," Fuchsia immediately corrected herself, "I didn't mean it like that! I meant 'oh,' as in... oh! I love you too!"

"Are you just saying that?" the Captain now became skeptical.

"No, I agree with you! It's just so unexpected. Out of all the human encounters I've heard about through friends or through my sisters, nothing like this was ever mentioned. You know, the part where the mermaid and the sailor fall in love? Typically the story ends in death, or running away at the last minute!"

"Oh, like I told you, I'm no sailor!" he chuckled, "I'm no captain either, I am the Captain. You'll never find anyone like me. And I can already tell, I'll never find anyone like you."

Fuchsia didn't want him to be right, but unfortunately, she knew he was.

"Hop on my ship!" he offered, "and I'll take you away!"

Fuchsia's heart skipped a beat. This was her dream -- to leave the mermaid world behind and run away with the love of her life.

But how was she to know he wasn't just another sailor with an evil plan to capture her? How was she supposed to believe that he was genuine -- or simply a sweet-talker? How naive would it be, to simply take his word? She was young enough to hope, but old enough to know better.

"I'd love to... but I can't."

"Well, why ever not?" he cried out.

"You're from the human world, I just can't trust you, I can't have faith that you won't take advantage and expose my entire species."

"You said it yourself, that you felt something! And you agreed, beyond logical explanation! I know we're not designed to love each other, or to even trust each other, but we have something here. This is true love. And if you let me go right now, I may never see you again, and you'll have to suffer the rest of your life knowing that I got away."

The more he urged, the more Fuchsia grew skeptical of his true intentions. Afterall, it seemed a little too easy for her to seduce him off his ship that smoothly. He must be playing her, she concluded.

"Captain," Fuchsia began, "it seems you've been stranded at sea for far too long. When was the last time you ate something? Or drank water?"

"Excuse me?" the Captain furrowed his eyebrows.

Fuchsia had heard it many times before: if you're in danger of being captured by a human, the best way out is to convince them that they're hallucinating, and that you're not real.

"I can't run away from you, for I am not real. There is no such thing as mermaids, silly. Now get back on your ship, stay hydrated, and try to find your way home as soon as possible!"

"Trust me, I know a real mermaid when I see one..." he sighed, displeased.

"Now let me swim to my mythical cave, and remember, I'm nonexistent. This is only a dream," Fuchsia continued her act. All those years of putting on shows for her town really sharpened her performance skills.

"Go on," he bowed his head in defeat. He wasn't buying it.

"I'll never forget this," Fuchsia confessed, before quickly adding, "but I'm not real."

The Captain hopped on his ship and didn't even wave goodbye before sailing away.

Fuchsia stood still in the water, watching her handsome Captain leave. She was assured in her decision to stay safe and keep her merpeople protected.

Yet still... he was already echoing through her mind like a broken record...

And now he was gone. Fuchsia would swim back home where she could relax. Deep down she had a feeling that this wasn't the last of him. She knew he'd be back very soon, she just knew it... right?

III. THE MERMAID BALL

A Party for the Hottest Sea People

It had been a long, agonizing six months since Fuchsia had first encountered the Captain face to face -- and they hadn't met ever since.

Fuchsia couldn't believe it: he was always on her mind, taking up space and living there rent-free. She tried so hard to distract herself but he was still stuck in her head. She flirted with many boys just to find herself wishing she was flirting with the Captain instead. The other boys were like children playing games for amusement. But the Captain was like fire -- capable of total alchemy.

She kept asking herself, where did he go? When would he come back? The question was not if, but when! For, this could not be the end of her romantic saga, it just couldn't be!

On occasion, Fuchsia would swim back to her rock: the original scene of the crime. She noticed the Captain sailing by on his ship every now and then. She could still spot him from afar. But he refused to come back to her. He continued sailing in circles, never coming close again like that one day.

Fuchsia told herself it was only a matter of time before he would grow weak and quit resisting her beauty. She wanted him to beg for her. And yet the passing of time made her doubt herself even more -- it was as if he wanted her to beg for him! Preposterous!

Fuchsia continued fighting against her pull towards the Captain. If he really wanted her, then he would fight for her, she convinced herself.

And then one day, Fuchsia sat on her rock waiting to spot the Captain sailing by -- and that's when she saw -- there was another woman with him on his ship! She splashed water on her face to make sure she wasn't dreaming. But it was true.

Sailing by, the Captain looked her in the eyes and wrapped his arm around the mystery lady, who had black hair. Fuchsia's heart shattered into a million pieces. Holding back her tears, she plunged herself back into the sea and swam away as fast as she could.

She thought, what an evil man! Sailing right past me just to show that he's with someone else! How dare he!

Rushing to get back home to her cave where she could cry her eyes out, she was halted by Finn.

"Whoa, whoa!" he stopped her, "since when did you join the track team? What are you in such a rush for?"

Fuchsia couldn't help but offer a polite smile at his lame attempt of making a clever joke.

Noticing her eyes watering up, Finn said, "you know you can talk to me about anything. Is something wrong?"

Normally Fuchsia would just brush him off, but feeling extra vulnerable, she decided to engage.

"I'm a little heartbroken, to be honest," she admitted.

"You? Heartbroken? Tell me what the idiot did, and I'll kick his ass!"

Fuchsia chuckled in discomfort, if only I could tell him the whole story, if only I could say he was human...

"It's nothing, it's just..." she struggled to get her words out properly.

"C'mon," he tilted his head, "I'm not going to judge."

"I better get home, my sisters are waiting," she attempted to excuse herself.

"I'm not letting you leave until you tell me what's up."

"Well," she sighed, "what do you do if a guy comes on to you, and then disappears, and then you spot him with another woman?"

"He's playing you."

"But..." she debated whether or not she should mention the phrase 'I love you' was said.

"Sometimes guys just like to flirt. I do it all the time. I'm sure you can find someone better."

Fuchsia decided to leave it at that, "you're right," she nodded.

"Now tell me, what's up with you and Marino?"

"Huh?"

"I've been seeing you two spending a lot of time together. He said he's taking you out tonight."

"Oh," she shrugged, "eh..."

"Look, if you're really hung up on this guy who's playing you, then what are you doing with Marino?"

"What does it matter to you?" she struck back.

"Because, you're like a sister to me. I want to look out for you."

Fuchsia smirked. She could trust Finn as far as she could throw him.

"I mean it," he insisted.

"Can I go home now?" she rolled her eyes.

"Maybe it's time you have a serious talk with Marino. Just make sure he's not stringing you along."

"Oh, I'm sure of it. He's crazy about me!"

"...or that it's not you who's stringing him along," he added.

Fuchsia paused. Maybe he had a point.

"Go on," he motioned, "get ready for your big date tonight."

Fuchsia prepared herself for a night out with Marino, but now Finn's words were stuck in her head. Perhaps it was time that the merpeople took her more seriously. She supposed she really should have a deep talk with Marino and get a better feel for their future.

So, she and Marino went out for sea cocktails. They sat at a bar and swayed along with the live music, a jazzy performance.

Thoughts of the Captain continued invading Fuchsia's head, but she pushed past them with as much resistance as she could. The Captain was gone now, she had to convince herself -- and if he truly loved her, he'd be with her -- not with that black-haired lady.

"Marino," Fuchsia began, "I was thinking about having a serious talk with you."

Marino gulped with hesitation, "serious? Can't we just enjoy our drinks?"

"That's what we always do," Fuchsia rolled her eyes and sighed with frustration.

"Well, what is it? What's going on?"

"I... I was thinking..." Fuchsia paused with shyness.

"C'mon now, spit it out!" He demanded with impatience.

"Let's talk about marriage!" She finally blurted out.

Just then, the merman sitting next to them slightly turned his head with his ears perked up, eavesdropping in on the conversation.

Marino was sinking down in his chair with embarrassment, "uh... what about it?"

Fuchsia pushed through, ignoring the awkwardness, "I mean, you've been chasing me for years! Don't you think it's time we make a commitment?"

"Maybe we can discuss it later."

"No!" Fuchsia denied, catching the attention of even more mermaids and mermen surrounding them.

Marino looked around, eyeing the crowd, silently pointing out that everyone seemed to be listening now.

"What?" Fuchsia was solely focused on Marino.

Marino remained quiet and uncomfortable, forcing Fuchsia to finally drop the subject and move on. The rest of the evening was mainly silent until Marino swam her home.

Leaning in to give her a kiss goodnight, Fuchsia stopped him.

"What was that all about?" She huffed.

"Huh? I always kiss you goodnight!"

"It's not that," she furrowed her eyebrows.

"Oh, earlier? At the bar?"

"Yes!" She screamed.

"I was caught off guard. Why speak about something so personal in public? Everyone could hear us."

"Marriage is a public thing. I thought we were on the same page. I thought you couldn't wait to tie me down. I didn't know you were ashamed of me..." Fuchsia looked down, tearing up.

"No!" Marino widened his eyes in panic, "of course we're on the same page! I never wanna lose you!"

"Then what is it?"

"I'm just not comfortable with everyone butting in on our business! I thought we had agreed to wait a little longer, till we're older. We've only just begun adulthood."

Fuchsia paused to think it over. Looking into Marino's eyes, she couldn't fully picture herself marrying him, at least not yet. But she certainly wanted to move forward.

"I just feel so stiff," she confessed, "I want to move forward. I want a new adventure!" She clenched her fists impatiently.

"We can have that together someday, I promise," he stared at her hopelessly, whimpering like a puppy-dog.

"Maybe some time apart might do," she hesitantly suggested.

"No!" He furiously shook his head, "I can't lose you, it would break my heart!"

Feeling defeated, Fuchsia said, "I'm tired. I'll see you tomorrow."

"Look, if you're mad, I just..." he began to explain himself.

But she stopped him, "it's fine, seriously! Let's drop it. I had a great night. Thank you."

The two said their goodbyes before Fuchsia returned to her family cave where her sisters resided.

Finally all alone, Fuchsia thought out loud with frustration, "I hate men! They chase you until you chase them back, and then they run!"

Out popped Fuchsia's three sisters, who were terribly nosey. She assumed that they were fast asleep by now, but of course, they were curious about how her date had gone.

Amber, the eldest, had fiery-red hair, which matched her fiery-red attitude. Her sassiness was almost out of control. Amber was the leader and decision-maker of the family. Amber and Fuchsia could relate to each other's short tempers and excitable passions.

Second eldest, Turquoise, had lavish, blue-green hair. Turquoise also held great responsibility. She was quite peaceful and passive, but still composed a bossy frame of mind. Both Turquoise and Fuchsia were guilty of being people-pleasers.

Youngest sister, Emerald, had been born a few years after Fuchsia. Her hair was as green as freshly cut grass on a spring day. Emerald was the quietest and shyest of the family, the introverted one who preferred keeping to herself. Fuchsia felt connected to Emerald's need for alone-time.

Fuchsia was very close with her sisters. As a famous actress who everyone adored, it was incredibly challenging for her to trust and open up to others. She had countless fans, but hardly any friends. Fuchsia was paranoid that by befriending her fans, and showing strangers her true colors, she would inevitably disappoint them with her hidden flaws and imperfections. She preferred being an actress, a mysterious chameleon who could fit the mold of any type of character, an interchangeable icon who could never be thoroughly analyzed.

With her sisters, Fuchsia couldn't keep any part of herself hidden from them -- they knew her far too well. They knew how emotional she was, how dramatic she was, and how skilled she was at hiding her true feelings. And most importantly, they let her keep up with this facade.

However, on the down side, Fuchsia's sisters loved her a little too much. They were fiercely protective, extremely critical, and overly bombarding.

"How was your date?" Amber asked.

The three sisters anxiously gathered around Fuchsia like groupies, desperate for some juicy gossip.

"It was..." Fuchsia sighed, "not great."

"Well, what happened?" Turquoise inquired.

"I don't wanna talk about it," Fuchsia dismissed her sisters, making her way to bed.

But her sisters wouldn't take 'no' for an answer.

"Are you taking Marino to the Mermaid Ball?" Amber continued.

The Mermaid Ball was approaching next week -- the biggest and hottest party for all mermaids, mermen, and other mystical sea creatures. This was the first year Fuchsia could attend, as she was finally of age. The party was reserved for those who were at least eighteen-years old.

"What a silly question," Turquoise commented, "of course they're going together!"

"Actually..." Fuchsia said reluctantly, "I'm not sure."

The sisters gasped in disbelief.

"Seriously?" Emerald widened her eyes, "you would go to a party without Marino?"

"Oh, Fuchsia!" Amber threw her arms up, "I think that's great! There's plenty of other mermen for you to choose from -- Finn, Reef, Gill, Oceanus, Archer, Coral, Pacifico..."

"This is my first ball," Fuchsia cut her off before she could list one more boy's name, "I feel like I need to do this alone. I'll just get there and see what happens!"

"Aha," Turquoise nodded, "good for you!"

"Who are you going with?" Fuchsia interrogated, staring at Amber and Turquoise.

"Oh, we're going alone, of course," Amber answered for the both of them, "just like every other year."

"We like it that way," Turquoise added, "it's more fun."

"Alright!" Fuchsia nodded, "then let me do the same!"

"It's just so unlike you," Turquoise explained, "you're into all the fairytale stuff, the whole concept of one man for life. And now that you're finally an adult, you've been saying lately how you're looking for commitment, something more serious."

"And you and Marino are like, obsessed with each other!" Amber threw in, "we always thought he'd be the one!"

"Nuh-uh," Fuchsia snarkily denied, "you two always told me that the fairytale fantasy is merely a dream, unrealistic."

"Yeah, yeah," Amber stuck out her tongue, "we're just teasing you."

"We know you're different," Turquoise said with insight, "you don't go along with society."

"If anyone can chase the fairytale, it's you!" Amber exclaimed.

"Yeah!" Emerald optimistically agreed.

Fuchsia felt a shift in perspective. Perhaps she had been taking her sister's teasing too seriously. Just because they didn't want to settle down, didn't mean she had to follow. Her sisters believed in her, no matter what path she followed. Suddenly a glimpse of hope entered her heart again. And that's when the Captain's face ran through her mind once more.

Laying down, attempting to fall asleep, Fuchsia could not stop thinking about the Captain. There was hope, afterall. She finally let herself believe that they could have a future together. Imagining his eyes on hers for the rest of their lives, she perceived the deepest level of intimacy that they could possibly reach.

All the mermen who were chasing after her -- it was all so shallow. They were attracted to her, but they weren't in love. They liked her beauty, her fame, and her cleverly crafted persona -- but none of them could see who she really was beyond the exterior of synthetic perfection.

The Captain, on the other hand, could penetrate through all of that. Although it seemed like they barely knew each other, Fuchsia could feel his spirit deep inside of her heart, as if a part of his soul had resided inside of her since birth. This connection was spiritual, existing far beyond the physical plane. Appearing as strangers in this material world, Fuchsia knew that they had been lovers in all of their previous lifetimes.

A heartening idea ran through her head -- that the Captain was using these past six months to build up the courage to meet her at the Mermaid Ball, where they could have that second chance to run away together. This time, Fuchsia was sure that she would accept him. There were no more doubts or trust issues. She knew that he was the one.

The Mermaid Ball would be the perfect opportunity for the two of them to reunite. Having those six months to figure out if he could be trusted or not, now Fuchsia could faithfully accept him as her destiny.

As her thoughts ran mad, Fuchsia decided to pray to Mother Mermaid. Goddess of the sea, Mother Mermaid was always watching after her merpeople with care. Never making her physical presence known, it was believed that she was always listening, and if you prayed to her for guidance, she would reward you with exactly what you needed.

"Mother Mermaid," Fuchsia began in prayer, "I do hope you are listening. I have realized that I am in love. I love the Captain. I know I love him, because I haven't been able to stop thinking about him, and I've never felt this way about anyone else before."

Going on, "Mother Mermaid, I do not ask for much, only this one, small favor. Can you help me unite with the Captain? I've tried waiting for him out on the rock, but all he does is sail right past me. If you could send him to the Mermaid Ball, that would be divine! I would be forever gracious for your mercy and kindness!"

Ending her prayer, in satisfaction, Fuchsia closed her eyes and swiftly dozed off.

IV. A CAPTAIN, OR A MAN OF TRICKS?

U pon sunrise, it seemed that Fuchsia's prayers had already been answered. There was a letter that had been mysteriously placed on her stomach. It was a folded piece of paper tied together with brown string.

A tingle in her bellybutton told her that it was from the Captain, but her brain quickly stepped in to remind herself that that would be impossible.

Examining the letter, Fuchsia untied the knot of yarn and unfolded the paper, revealing this message:

"Dear Fuchsia, I haven't stopped thinking about you. Let's meet at The Mermaid Ball and continue our love story... Love, Captain."

It was the Captain! He did this! He wrote her a love letter and sent it to her!

"Mother Mermaid!" Fuchsia squealed with joy, "thank you, thank you, thank you!"

Wholeheartedly frazzled, her stomach fluttered. There were so many questions. *How did he send me this letter? How did he find me? How does he know about The Mermaid Ball? Is someone playing a joke on me -- but who else knows about the Captain?*

Her head was spinning. What a rollercoaster of emotions. One moment she was feeling hopeless and the next, she was full of faith. The only constant that remained was 'confusion.'

Surely, she couldn't tell her sisters about this letter.

Fuchsia wondered if perhaps Marino, or Finn, or any other jealous boy, had been spying on her. If this note truly came from the Captain, then he must have some sort of magical power that allowed this letter to fall into her lap so randomly, she concluded.

Her prayer from the night before was no coincidence. Perhaps, the Captain had Mother Mermaid's magical powers to assist him in delivering this letter.

She determined that there was only one way to find out -- show up at The Mermaid Ball and wait for him.

That night, Fuchsia primed and polished herself to perfection. She curled her pink locks, dolled up her face, plucked her eyebrows and filed her nails, and then she put on her favorite seashell bra along with a lavish, rose gold necklace.

Mermaids didn't wear clothing -- just seashell bras and jewelry, while mermen simply wore jewelry and that was all. Yet another reason why commitment was so rare among merpeople -- they all flaunted their beauty.

Over and over, Fuchsia told herself that the Captain would not be there – followed by a tiny whisper that he would. She was trying to keep her hopes down, but the little glimpse of faith inside her heart could not be ignored.

Fuchsia looked at her reflection in a crystal and told herself, "just relax. If he's there, then it will be great. If he's not, then it will still be great. No expectations. No disappointment."

Older sisters Amber and Turquoise had gone ahead without her, snagging VIP tickets to the pre-party. They invited her, but she declined, preferring to go alone so that she would have a better chance at spotting the Captain – *if he even shows up, that is.*

Fuchsia was typically a highly confident young lady, but tonight, her confidence was shaking. She had to gather more bravery than she naturally had. For a quick second, she entertained the thought of ditching the ball entirely and snuggling up so safely in her little cave all night. But no – she was going to be brave, she convinced herself.

Once she arrived at the party, she instantly felt a sinking in her gut. It felt like she didn't belong, like she was meant to turn around and go back home. Her intuition was telling her something. Yet she pushed past the discomfort and forced herself to keep going.

Scanning the crowd, she searched for her Captain.

Where would he be? Who would he be talking to?

Yet he was nowhere in sight. She told herself that he must be running late, that he must be building the suspense, trying to make her sweat.

Fuchsia stood alone, figuring it would be easier this way for the Captain to approach her. But after waiting for so long, she felt incredibly awkward standing there all by herself. So, she sought out her older sisters.

She found them by the bar, drinking sea cocktails. She decided to cling to them for the remainder of the night until the Captain showed up.

Time passed and Fuchsia's ambition was withering away. Her eyes were glued to the entrance. *Any moment now...*

A man tapped Fuchsia on the shoulders. She turned around in anticipation of greeting the Captain, just to be severely disappointed – it was some random merman.

"Hi, I'm Arctico, from the North," he introduced himself, "I don't believe we've met."

"Uh... hi," Fuchsia greeted with falter, "I'm Fuchsia."

"Care to dance?"

"Sorry, I'm waiting for my date."

"Oh, I see," he nodded, "good luck on your date," he smiled politely before finding another mermaid to hit on.

"A date?" Turquoise quickly spun her head around like an owl, "so you *did* invite Marino?"

"No!" Fuchsia immediately shook her head.

"Then who?" Turquoise inquired, "Finn? Gill? Archer?"

Amber, finishing up a conversation with another merman, quickly joined in with, "am I missing out on boy-talk?"

Fuchsia sunk in her seat, mortified by the incessant nosiness of her sisters. But with her hope running thin, she felt no choice but to let go of resistance.

So she admitted, "okay, it's true, I am waiting for a date... but you'd never guess who."

"A mystery merman?" Amber raised her eyebrows seductively.

"Eh... not exactly..." Fuchsia ground her teeth in anxiety. There was no point in hiding the truth from her sisters. They always had her best interest at heart, aside from her fear of their judgment. Plus, they were bound to find out soon enough.

"What are we missing?" Turquoise asked.

With coyness, Fuchsia confessed, "I met a, uh... Captain."

"A captain?!" Both sisters nearly shouted as Fuchsia tried to shush them.

"I know, I know," Fuchsia covered her face, "I'm an idiot!"

"How scandalous!" the sisters agreed.

To Fuchsia's surprise, they were less angry, and far more amused.

"Aren't you gonna yell at me?" Fuchsia pouted.

"Sweetie, you're an adult now," Amber consulted, "you're allowed to make your own stupid mistakes... oh, did I say 'stupid mistakes?' I meant, uh, 'choices,' yeah, choices." Clearly she was a few sea cocktails in by now.

Giggling, Turquoise added, "hey, captains are quite handsome, how could we blame ya?"

Fuchsia forced a smile.

"But all jokes aside," Turquoise continued, "you have to be careful. Humans can't be trusted, you know."

"Wait," Amber recollected herself, "is this Captain-dude actually coming here -- to meet you at this party?"

"Supposedly," Fuchsia nodded with caution.

"You know they'll never let him in, right?" Amber said.

"Is he, like, wearing a disguise or something?" Turquoise asked.

"How did you meet this man, anyway?" Amber asked.

"How long have you two known each other?" Turquoise asked.

"I don't know!" Fuchsia threw her hands in the air, completely overwhelmed, "all I know is that one day I swam to the surface, met the Captain, we shared a moment of passion until I pushed him away, and then he was distant ever since, even sailing the sea right past me with some black-haired lady! But then I woke up this morning and a letter magically appeared on my lap, and it was written from him, saying he would be here tonight!" And then she breathed out heavily with exhaustion.

After a short pause, Amber responded with, "all I can say is, be careful."

"But don't you think it's strange that his letter just magically appeared in my lap?" Fuchsia asked, "don't you think he could be... magic?"

"The human world is very strange," Turquoise said.

"Human or not, I wouldn't trust him," Amber said, "just enjoy yourself tonight, okay? Don't spend the whole time staring at the entrance. There's plenty of mermen here to have fun with."

With reluctance, Fuchsia agreed. She felt slightly better after confiding in her sisters, like a weight had been lifted off her shoulders. And yet, it only seemed to be replaced with the weight of loneliness.

A few sea cocktails later and Fuchsia grew terribly impatient. Once the clock struck midnight, the entrance gate had closed, and she knew that he was definitely not going to show.

Suddenly Fuchsia's face turned as pink as her hair. She felt like the biggest idiot in the shore. Everyone around her was smiling, laughing, and dancing, having a great time — while Fuchsia was struggling to hold back tears.

The mermaids and mermen were so caught up in their own joy that nobody, not even her sisters, noticed Fuchsia sneaking out and making her way back home. She cried, and cried, and cried.

Sadness quickly turned into an anger she had never known before. She cursed the Captain, cursed the world, but mainly cursed herself. Fuchsia screamed at the top of her lungs, a loudness she never even knew she was capable of.

"I CURSE YOU, CAPTAIN!" she wailed with all her might, "YOU ARE THE DEVIL!"

Caught up in so much rage, she created a massive hurricane that disturbed the entire ocean. The ground shook along with her trembling body.

Youngest sister, Emerald, rushed to her side.

"What's going on?" Emerald panicked, groggily waking up from her sleep.

"Please don't tell our older sisters about this," Fuchsia begged with desperation and embarrassment, "they warned me and I should have known."

"Known about what? What happened?"

"I did something bad," Fuchsia looked down with shame, "I swam to the surface of the sea and I fell for a dashing Captain. He promised me that he'd meet me here tonight, but he never showed."

"Aww, I'm so sorry," Emerald sympathized.

"Don't feel bad, I deserve this."

"Do Amber and Turquoise know?"

"I told them the background story and they told me to 'be careful.' I just didn't mention the part where I completely fell for him. It's a little too late now for 'careful.'"

Emerald nodded, and then curiously questioned, "why is this hitting you so hard?"

"I just... I just..." Fuchsia struggled to put the words together, still in tears, "I just... didn't think I cared this much."

The two sisters hugged each other in silence.

Heading to her bed, Fuchsia once again prayed to Mother Mermaid -- "what happened?" She cried to her goddess hopelessly, "you were supposed to bring us together..."

All night, Fuchsia could hardly sleep. There was no way that anyone else could have sent her that letter, for she hadn't yet told anyone about the Captain before that moment. The only possibility was if someone had been spying on her and decided to play a joke -- but her mermaid radar was very strong, and she believed she would've sensed if it was anyone else. The Captain was the only man for her, and he was magic, pure magic.

What's the sense in waiting for him to sail by again? It was now her turn to profess her love to him. Afterall, he had given his heart to her completely, and she totally took it for granted. Lesson had been learned. He wanted her to realize how much she truly loved him and needed him, she concurred.

Early that next morning, at the crack of dawn, Fuchsia packed a suitcase and attempted to leave home before sunrise. Yet of course, right as she was leaving home, Amber and Turquoise were returning from the party.

"Fuchsia!" they stopped her, "where are you going?"

"I'm going to find the Captain!" she firmly announced.

"What?!" they gasped.

"There's something here and I'm sick of fighting it. I'm going to give him my all. No more waiting around. I'm coming for him!"

"No!" both sisters cried out.

"You can't stop me!" Fuchsia barked back.
"We told you to be careful!" Amber shouted, "this is not careful!"

"'Careful' is out the window! 'Careful' is what caused this whole heartache in the first place! Get out of here with your 'careful!'" Fuchsia exclaimed.

"Ex-*squooze* me!?" Amber drunkenly slurred.

Buzzed with sea cocktails and sleep-deprived, the older sisters struggled to keep their balance.

Jumping out of bed once again, youngest sister Emerald rushed in to save the scene.

"Amber! Turquoise!" Emerald said, trying to calm everyone down, "Let's get you two to bed! You've been out all night long!" And then she grabbed Fuchsia's arm, "I'll stay with Fuchsia, okay?"

Nodding, the two older sisters crashed into their beds and practically fell into a coma.

"Whew!" Emerald sighed with relief, "I was afraid you ladies were about to get into a fist fight!"

Fuchsia was speechless. Her quiet and meek little sister had taken charge for the first time in her life. She didn't even know what to expect next.

"Okay, they're asleep now," Emerald smiled, "now go find your Captain!"

Stunned, Fuchsia excitedly nodded.

"Oh, Emerald!" she cheered, "why is the youngest always the wisest?"

"Quick!" Emerald demanded, "before they wake up!"

Off and away, Fuchsia swam as fast as she could. She headed straight towards the volcanic mountain -- the little rock sticking out of the water. She scanned the sea... no ship in sight.

Using her mental powers, she closed her eyes and sent a message to her Captain.

"Dear Captain… I can no longer hide my true feelings for you… I love you! Now meet me at the rock -- for real this time -- and we can genuinely continue our love story… Love always, Fuchsia."

And as soon as she opened her eyes, there it was -- the ship. And on this ship, was the Captain.

He pulled out his binoculars. Once again, he was headed her way at full speed, looking her dead in the eyes. He was coming for her. Fuchsia grinned so wide that her face muscles cramped.

Picking up speed, he still wasn't moving fast enough, she thought.

"C'mon, c'mon…" Fuchsia said to herself in anticipation.
Above her, more birds flew by. Fuchsia joined them, spreading her wings, ready to fly to the love of her life, and have her happily ever after. To her, there was no greater freedom than that.
"Fly on, birds!" Fuchsia told her feathery friends, "But don't just go with the wind! Follow your heart!"

The ship came closer and closer. Fuchsia was ready to jump right on. Sliding off the rock, she began swimming his way.
Curiously, the Captain did not lay down his anchor. Instead, he continued to keep on sailing.

"Captain?" she shouted out with puzzlement.

Still sailing, the ship rode right past her.

"Does he not see me?" she asked herself.

Continuing to sail away, Fuchsia spotted a woman's head pop

out. She looked different from the black-haired woman -- her hair was bright red. She watched in absolute shock and disgust as the Captain put his arm around her.

Clenching her fists and revealing her fangs, Fuchsia was absolutely livid. And yet, peculiarly enough, a part of her was not even surprised...

"Your letter was revenge," she quietly stated to herself, "you were upset because I rejected you, and now it was your turn to be the one to reject me..."

And then the ship was gone.

"So, you're not a Captain after all," she muttered to herself, "you're a man of tricks."

The fog in her brain began to slowly lift as she faced the reality of his deception. It was no longer true love. She could now see her dream world for what it was — just a dream.

V. TO BE A MERMAID

(What Does It Mean?)

Many more months later, Fuchsia had fallen into a deep and dark depression. She stopped dancing, singing, acting, and socializing altogether. Her once pink hair had now turned grey and dry, her complexion was as pale as a ghost, dark shadows stained under her eyes, and her bones had become brittle.

She still couldn't help but swim to her rock here and there -- to spot the Captain once again sailing by, who's ship was becoming more and more blurry, as his distance grew further. He would still pass by, but never close enough for her to see his face. Sometimes it seemed like another figure was standing next to him, but it was too far for her to clearly see.

On her nineteenth birthday, after spending the bulk of her time sulking in her bedroom, her sisters demanded that she put on another show. She used to perform every week, but now she was too depressed. Her sisters, worried sick, made several threats if she wouldn't put on a show for her birthday -- they would stop bringing her food, they would pull her out of their cave home by force, or worst of all: they would invite Marino in!

"I don't want to see anyone!" Fuchsia screamed.

Fuchsia's sisters were insistent that putting on a show again would help her get her mojo back. They knew how much she adored entertaining others, making them laugh, watching them cheer her on.

"But Fuch," Turquoise sympathized, "it's your birthday! You can't be miserable today. Acting is your favorite, it's the only way to kick you out of this funk."

"Your butt is gonna be on that stage in five minutes," Amber demanded, "we already told the whole village -- they're waiting for you!"

"Seriously?" Fuchsia rolled her eyes with a sigh, "you already promised them a show?"

"You don't wanna let them down now, do you?" Amber nudged.

"Ugh!" Fuchsia clenched her fists, "fine, I'll do it!"

So, with dread, Fuchsia subordinately headed towards the stage (a large rock) as all the mermaids and mermen gathered around, anticipating yet another spectacle from their star. It was time to perform.

Rummaging through the crowd, no one could even recognize her without her vivid, pink hair. Now brokenhearted, she looked completely different -- as if she had aged several centuries within the course of a few months.

"Where's Fuchsia?" someone screamed out as she stood there facing the crowd.

"Excuse my appearance," she brushed it off, "it's all a part of the costume," she improvised.

"WOO!!!" Her sisters forcibly screamed, attempting to cheer her on. It was cringeworthy.

Her voice had weakened and it felt much harder to speak. Those in the back were pushing themselves closer, struggling to hear.

The original plan was to put on a play she had composed herself -- about a beautiful princess who was rescued by a daring knight. She came up with this story the night of The Mermaid Ball, as boredom had struck her while she was waiting for the Captain to show up -- but never did.

Yet as soon as she hit the stage, feeling much more like an ugly monstress, that wouldn't do anymore. She could not bear to tell a fairytale of courtly love. Instead, she would have to take a completely different route.

Doing her best to stay in character, Fuchsia performed "Little Red Riding Hood" from the grandma's perspective. She was doing okay, and the crowd was buying her act -- until about halfway through, when she turned completely frozen and burst into tears. She could barely keep it together. Visions of the Captain with another woman kept playing through her head.

"To be continued!" she announced before rushing off the stage in hysterics.

"Wow!" Gill stopped her, "such a beautiful performance, Fuchsia," he smiled with awe, "your crying looks so convincing."

"Thank you," Fuchsia could hardly whisper.

"Where have you been? We've all missed you, so dearly." It was unlike Gill to be so forward, which took Fuchsia aback.

"Oh," Fuchsia fibbed on the spot, unable to be honest about her heartache, "working on my creative arts," she sighed.

"You know, the show is over, silly," he smirked, "you can be your bubbly self again."

"I'm just so committed to the character," she lied, "once you're in that mindset, it's hard to snap out of it."

"Aha," he slowly nodded.

Being in public was so stressful for Fuchsia. She felt like she always had to be happy, because that's what made others happy. Even when she could not conceal her depression, she still managed to find a way -- by pretending it was an act.

"Ugh!" Fuchsia was now gaining strength as her sorrow turned into frustration, "that wolf! That big, bad wolf! How dare he play such evil tricks! How dare he!" She stomped her tail against the sand floor.

"Oh goodness, you really *are* dedicated to the character," Gill widened his eyes -- impressed, but also a little alarmed.

"I suppose I deserve it," she moaned, "wasting half a year, going on dates and entertaining others, only throwing myself at him until after I saw him with someone else."

"Huh?" Gill paused, totally lost, "are we still talking about the fable?"

"Uh," Fuchsia caught herself, "maybe I have a few plot holes to sew up. I better go work on that before next week's performance. Excuse me..."

"Sure..." Gill furrowed his eyebrows.

Finally returning home, Fuchsia let herself fall completely apart.

"Fuchsia!" her sisters shouted as they came back, "what a performance!"

"Too bad it's my last," she scowled.

"What are you talking about?" Amber asked, "and what happened to you?" She ran her fingers through Fuchsia's grey, brittle, straw hair. And then she placed her hand on her arm, noticing her weak bones and absolute depletion of muscle.

"We miss your pink hair," Emerald moaned.

Turquoise questioned, "is this all because of a stupid captain?"

"Not a captain, *THEE* Captain," Fuchsia abruptly corrected.

"This dude just sounds like a jerk!" Amber declared, "forget about him!"

"Yeah," Turquoise agreed, "that's no reason to give up on being a mermaid."

And then something struck Fuchsia at her very core. *What did it even mean 'to be a mermaid,' anyway? Was there any point?*

"Can I just have some space?" Fuchsia whined.

"You've been asking for space for a while now," Amber ground her teeth, "I'm telling you, what you need is to get yourself out there! Keep putting on more shows! Go out on dates again! Meet new mermen!"

"I don't care about any of that!" Fuchsia shook her head profusely, "what's the point?"

"That's your depression speaking," Turquoise assumed, "once you start having fun again, you'll snap out of that pessimism! You won't be thinking such gloomy thoughts."

"These are *real* thoughts," Fuchsia defended, "how much fun can a mermaid have before she craves something deeper?"

"Deeper, like what?" Emerald tilted her head.

"Like..." Fuchsia took a long breath.

"Don't say 'the Captain!'" Amber ferociously cut in.

"Maybe it's not about him," Fuchsia said with softness, "even before we met, I felt this empty hollowness in my heart. I felt like I was living my life on autopilot, swimming in circles day after day, never getting anywhere. Life became so safe and comfortable.

"Where is the adventure? Where is that feeling that makes your heart thump and your body tremble? I know it's out there. And I'm not talking about that 'high' that comes and goes, I'm talking about a yearning from your soul that grows even stronger with time."

"Hmm," Amber nodded slowly, "I think I know what you mean. You meet a guy, you have an amazing date together, he's a great kisser, sparks are flying... and then a few weeks later, you're sick of him! So you find another merman -- but it's all the same!"

"Or," Turquoise interrupted, "you go out dancing, you drink tons of sea cocktails, you feel so free... but then the next morning, you wake up feeling like crap, with the world's worst headache! And then, that night, you go out and do it again!"

"Oh!" Emerald giggled, eager to chime in, "you feast on really delicious fish, and it tastes so good, but then you get a horrible bellyache."

"Exactly!" Fuchsia threw her hands up.

"Well, that's life!" Amber exclaimed, "what goes up, must come down... and then back up again!"

"Ugh," Fuchsia hoffed in frustration. *"Not* what I was getting at..." Her sisters couldn't understand. What she was feeling inside was impossible to accurately convey.

"I'm telling you the same thing I told Turquoise when she became an adult," Amber lectured, "don't fall in love. And if you do, you better be sure that the merman loves you far more than you love him back."

"Yeah, it's true," Turquoise agreed, "mermaids have fragile hearts and we have to protect ourselves."

"Don't you think mermen have fragile hearts too?" Fuchsia defended.

Amber and Turquoise bursted into a fit of laughter.

"All mermen are total *sardines!*" Amber snorted, "all they care about is what you look like."

"Mm-hmm," Turquoise added with smugness, "they want a pretty mermaid and that's all. Total slime-bags."

"I'm only sixteen, and I already knew that," Emerald sassily smirked.

The three sisters, Amber, Turquoise, and Emerald, fell into a pit of laughter. Meanwhile, Fuchsia shook her head.

Fuchsia sighed, "you ladies are only making me feel worse."

"The sooner you accept the facts of life, the happier you'll be," Amber persuaded.

"I won't accept it," Fuchsia denied, "there has to be more to life than an endless cycle of quick thrills with inevitable come-downs…"

"You're overthinking it all, Fuch," Turquoise told her, "learn how to go with the flow and ride the waves."

"But what about the humans!?" Fuchsia bursted, "are we simply going to let them crash and burn? What if that's what our purpose is, as merpeople, to save them?"

"The humans are a total lost cause," Amber stated.

Turquoise agreed, "yeah, it's better that the humans destroy themselves, rather than destroy us."

"I think we're spoiled down here, with our safe and predictable lifestyles. I think we all jump from merman to merman, or mermaid to mermaid, or one sea cocktail to the next sea cocktail, as a distraction from the painful truth that we were designed to have purpose. It doesn't sit right with me -- the thought of life being so pleasurable. There's no growth without the storm, no real reward without the challenge! There just has to be more to life than swimming in circles all day long!"

And then there was silence. The three sisters had tried their best, and nothing was making Fuchsia come alive again. They thought, if she couldn't accept life as a mermaid, then they would have to accept her denial... at least for now. So they let her be for the night, determined to try again tomorrow morning.

As they swam off, Fuchsia nodded down in prayer. This time, she came to Mother Mermaid with more than one simple request -- this time, a full-on confessional.

"Mother Mermaid, although you have not answered my prayers of uniting with the Captain, I still believe you are listening. Let me make myself much more clear this time.

"I have lived nineteen years now as a mermaid. And it hasn't brought me any sense of meaning or purpose. I've experienced joy, fun, and laughter aplenty... and yet, I haven't grown. I still feel like a child.

"I want to be in love. I've flirted with many boys, had many crushes, but nothing like love. I have felt the burning desire of lust, followed by its painful aftertaste. I have played every game in the book. I have never truly let these walls down, always guarded myself with heavy armor, and still managed to get brutally destroyed.

"I fear that the depths of these oceans are still far too shallow for me. Everyone here is playing it safe, gorging themselves in pleasure... no one wants to take a chance, no one wants to risk it all... all the mermen chase me, but none of them have genuinely fought for me...

"I have suffered long enough! Take me away, please! Take me away!" Fuchsia tilted her head backwards and shot her arms up towards the sky.

Suddenly, swirls of stars danced around her body, lifting her off the bed, until she dissipated into a new world. She inhaled deeply with anxiety, contracting every muscle with tightness.

Letting out a great exhale, she found herself facing -- the one and only -- *Mother Mermaid*!

"Mother Mermaid, is it you?" Fuchsia stared in awe.

Looking around, there was no one else. Just the two of them. And deep-blue darkness of the ocean.

"It is I," she spoke in an overpowering, yet calming, voice. Her gentle features and youthful face made her appear to be as young as a nineteen-year old, like Fuchsia herself -- it was absurd to believe that this goddess was actually thousands of years old!

"Am I dreaming?" Fuchsia couldn't believe it.

"No, dear. You are very much awake."

"Wow," she was speechless, "y-you're r-real," she stuttered nervously.

"Of course I'm real!" Mother Mermaid barked, which caused Fuchsia to jump back in fear. "Why wouldn't I be real?"

"Well," Fuchsia gulped, attempting to explain herself, "no one has ever seen you before in person like this. Are you sure I'm not dreaming -- or dead?"

"You are very much awake!" Mother Mermaid repeated herself, this time sounded a bit more irritated.

"I'm sorry!" Fuchsia raised her eyebrows, "b-but... you didn't answer my prayer."

"What makes you say that?"

"I prayed to you, I asked you to unite the Captain and me at the mermaid ball. But he never showed up."

"My child, I'm working on it. Divine timing is at hand and you are going to have to wait."

"Huh?" Fuchsia's face lit up with hope as she felt her heart beat faster, "you're *working on it*?"

Like a therapist, Mother Mermaid calmly and curiously asked, "is there something you would like to confess?"

Being surrounded by such holiness and purity, Fuchsia immediately became hyper-aware of her sins. Mother Mermaid's radiance was glowing so strongly that her image was somewhat blurred, overpowered by her light. She was practically the same size as her, but something about her presence made her size seem so much greater than it actually was.

Fuchsia responded, bowing her head, "gee, Mother Mermaid. I feel so small and imperfect standing right next to you like this. It's no wonder you keep your image out of sight."

Mother Mermaid warmly smiled, "I know all -- there is nothing you can hide from me. So tell me how you feel -- like you were doing just before, in prayer. Yet this time, go deeper. Tell me everything. This time you know for sure that I am here listening. And I can help you."

Fuchsia had never felt so vulnerable in her life. She was an actress -- forcing herself into character was all she knew. Even with her sisters seeing another side of her, no one had ever figured out who the true Fuchsia really was. And now, facing Mother Mermaid, there was absolutely nowhere to hide. She could make light of her feelings, she could deny the truth as much as she wanted, but no matter what, Mother Mermaid was capable of seeing right through her.

"Well," Fuchsia attempted to begin, struggling to get out the words, "I'm-I'm sick of being a mermaid. I don't deserve to be one."

"I'm seeing guilt," Mother Mermaid observed, "tell me why you look so guilty."

"I do feel guilty," Fuchsia nodded in agreement, "I feel so much pressure to be something that I'm not."

"And what do you feel pressured to be?"

"I feel pressured to be a mermaid -- this beautiful, euphoric, fantasy-like mermaid. I always have to smile, I always have to be happy, and I always have to pretend I'm emotionless. To me, it's such a shallow way of living -- eat, sleep, party, repeat -- what can I gain from all that? There's a whole world out there -- *the human world* -- and we just sit back and mind our own business, basking in our glory while they decay in their suffering, awaiting their inevitable destruction so that we can collect their jewels and goodies while they struggle to start all over again."

"Mm-hmm," Mother Mermaid nodded.

Fuchsia carried on, "so, I did something bad. I took a chance. I swam to the surface of the sea and sat myself on a rock above the water. And that's when a ship came sailing by -- and on that ship, was a captain -- but not just any captain, it was *thee Captain.*" Her eyes widened.

"Yes..."

"It was love at first sight. And he gave me the chance to run away with him -- but I refused. I couldn't trust him. But looking back, I would've jumped on that ship in a heartbeat -- even if it meant murder, or the exploitation of my entire species -- I don't care! I'd do anything just for a chance with him. And that chance is gone. I blew it."

"I see you go back to that rock almost every day. And I see him sail past you all the time."

"He always sails right past me. He'll never lay his anchor down and approach me like he first did. I must've broken his heart, and now he only wants revenge. That's why he sent me that letter promising me he'd be at the mermaid ball," and then she asked, "wait -- how did he send me that letter, anyway? Or was it you?"

"Oh, child," Mother Mermaid sympathized -- nearly in a condescending way, "surely, you must realize now that the Captain is far more than human."

Fuchsia raised an eyebrow, speechless.

Mother Mermaid explained, "he has far more magic than meets the eye."

"What does that mean? He must be human -- he had the legs and everything! If not, then what is he?"

"That's beside the point," Mother Mermaid avoided, "Fuchsia, do you not see how blessed you are to be standing directly in front of me, having a full-on back and forth conversation? There is a reason for this. I have chosen you to fulfill an important destiny. You are a key part of the plan for world peace and love."

"I am?" Fuchsia was dumbfounded, still imagining this whole thing must be some sort of lucid dream.

"Yes!" Mother Mermaid excitedly exclaimed, "and this is your first assignment."

"My first assignment?"

"I'm sending you to the human world, as a human. And you are not welcome back until you can explain to me what it means to be a mermaid."

"Wh-what?" Fuchsia gulped, "this sounds like some sort of punishment."

"Not at all," Mother Mermaid denied, "you said you were craving a challenge -- well here it is!"

"What does this have to do with the Captain?" Fuchsia panicked.

"Soon enough, you will see everything fall into place and come together. If you truly want to accept the Captain as your destiny -- and all the mystical adventures this difficult road comes with -- you have to show me bravery."

"I'm nervous," Fuchsia admitted.

"I will grant you partial mermaid abilities, so that way you can still survive. It's going to be strenuous, rough, and very challenging."

"No!" Fuchsia begged, "I heard it's scary out there!"

"Indeed," she agreed.

Falling down into a kneel and teary-eyed, Fuchsia screamed, "please don't make me do this. I'm so sorry -- for putting the merpeople species at risk, for being so reckless, for refusing to appreciate my safety..."

And then Mother Mermaid's stern aura softened as she let out a smile.

"I believe in you," she assured her.

An unexpected wave of relief flowed through Fuchsia's body. It seemed like a punishment, but it wasn't. This was everything Fuchsia had been desiring. Yet now that it was actually becoming her new reality, she feared it. How perplexing the mind is, she thought.

"Okay," Fuchsia finally nodded with graciousness and bravery.

"Now go out there, be brave, and show me what it really means to be a mermaid!"

And just like that, Mother Mermaid set her free into the human world.

VI. WELCOME TO THE TWISTED WORLD

of Humanity!

With the blink of an eye, Fuchsia found herself in a beach town on an empty boardwalk where she still had a beautiful sight of the ocean. It was early sunrise, with no one else around.

She screamed out loud when she looked down and noticed her new human legs, painfully aware of them. They felt much heavier and squishier than her sleek tail. And then she wiggled her toes around, poking out of her flip flops, widening her eyes in madness. Sticking out her hands, she observed that her toes were just like mini-fingers. She could move them around, but with far less control than she could with her actual fingers.

No longer dressed in nothing but a seashell bra, Fuchsia was now covered up in a white, cotton sundress. The spaghetti straps comfortably hugged her shoulders, while the rest of the dress flowed upon her body, hugging her waist tightly. She ran her fingers through her hair to see it was a bit more voluminous, but still a greyish-brown color.

Fuchsia knew she couldn't stand there frozen forever. It was time to walk. Picking up her legs, she winced in agony, for the gravity of air was much heavier than the weightless water she used to swim through with ease. Like a toddler learning to walk, she attempted moving forward without losing her balance.

With each step, she adjusted, and swiftly enough she was walking like a natural. She walked and walked, her heart bursting with joy and delight. Now she was swaying her arms. It was so freeing!

However, it wasn't long before she grew tired and decided to take a rest on a wooden bench. Now that the humans were starting to emerge, Fuchsia could begin to study them. She simply sat there, wide-eyed, observing every person who walked by.

There were adorable children running around with their tired parents screaming after them. The little kids waddled, desperate for balance, as if they too had been merpeople who's tails were suddenly taken away from them. It made Fuchsia giggle with admiration.

There were teens and adults, glued to their cell phones. During her mermaid childhood, Fuchsia had heard many fables about cell phones and their human attachment. What's known as *"cell phones"* by the humans are referred to as *"personal robots"* by the merpeople.

She was taught that, due to mankind's incompetence, they all began to rely on personal robots. With the progression of their personal robots, came the decline of their sanity. And since the invention of these personal robots, their apocalyptic fate was right around the corner. It was only a matter of a few centuries or so before they'd be reliving the Atlantas era -- a robotic world full of complete human isolation.

There were declining elders just trying to keep up. Although their brains were clearly not as sharp and alert, there was something about these elders that made them seem more connected to reality than the young adults and teens. Perhaps, Fuchsia inferred, it was because they once lived before "the age of personal robots" -- mankind's stepping stone for technological slavery.

Right away, she determined the separation between humans and merpeople: distraction. Everyone was in such a hurry to go nowhere. They walked so fast as if they were running late for something, then stood still for a decent amount of time -- waiting for food, eating their food, chatting with one another, or twiddling their thumbs on their phones -- and then rushing off somewhere else to go stand still again. So much restlessness. No one could focus on one thing for too long.

After hours and hours of sitting on a boardwalk bench, trying to examine her subjects, Fuchsia realized that she would have to take a more intimate approach. It was all so overwhelming, especially with the boardwalk becoming more and more clustered with the passing of time. If she really wanted to study human nature, it would be best to deal with one person at a time.

That's when Fuchsia spotted a boy of who she guessed to be of similar age, with a glistening aura that stood out from all the rest. Her intuition was much weaker now, but she still felt a strong energy, a gravitational pull towards him.

"Excuse me," she approached the boy.

"Yeah?" He politely greeted.

"Sir, do you mind if I follow you around, and occasionally take notes?" Fuchsia inquired.

Speechless, he gave her an uncomfortable smile that turned into awkward laughter.

"I'll be quiet, you won't even know I'm here," she persuaded, noticing his hesitance. "Although, I'm sure I'll have a few questions -- if that's okay."

"Uhh," he stuttered, unsure of how to respond, "what do you mean?"

"I have an important assignment to complete and you could really help me out."

"Like a school project?"

"Sure! It's about mer..." she quickly caught herself, "it's about, uh, sea men!"

He burst out into more laughter.

"It's actually a very serious matter, but I appreciate your humor," she shrugged.

"Sure, you can follow me home and I can guarantee you an A-plus," he joked.

"It's not graded: it's either a pass or a fail. But if I could go home with you, then that would be great!"

"So, um, how much have you had to drink?" He asked, looking around anxiously.

"Like, ocean water? Or sea cocktails?"

The boy stared at her in confusion as Fuchsia took notice of the paranoid and untrusting nature of humans.

"Are you out here all alone?"

"I mean," Fuchsia looked around, puzzled, "there's many, many humans here. Can't you see them all?" She pointed out with her finger.

"Is there someone you can call? Where's your phone?"

"I don't have a phone."

"Where are you staying? Are you lost? Can I walk you home?"

"*This* is my new home!" She threw her hands up towards the sky.

"Well, where are you sleeping tonight?" The boy was growing frustrated.

"I dunno," Fuchsia carelessly shrugged, "on the beach?"

"You're not serious," he smirked.

Fuchsia sighed in agitation, now she was growing frustrated too, "why doesn't anyone take me seriously!?"

Just then, a friend of the boy walked over, chomping down on a basket of fries and sipping on a paper bagged drink.

"This girl is totally wasted," the boy explained to his friend, "she ain't got no friends with her, no phone... she's telling me she's sleeping on the beach tonight."

"I'm not drunk," Fuchsia defended herself.

"Dude, she's not drunk," the other guy pointed out, "look at her pupils, she's on some weird drug. She's gone."

"Am not!" Fuchsia insisted, clenching her fists.

"She doesn't even have a place to sleep," the boy continued explaining to his friend.

"I told you, I can sleep on the sand!" She placed her hands on her hips.

"Just take her back to the hotel!" The boy's friend insisted.

"She's gonna wake up tomorrow and have no memory of this."

"Just bring her back, c'mon."

"Look, I don't want to take advantage of you," the first boy turned and looked at Fuchsia.

"What are you talking about?" Fuchsia said, "you'd be doing me a favor. This is a very important assignment. I mean, I guess I can find someone else to research…"

"Hold up," the second guy said, "you can research me tonight instead."

"Wait," the first guy stopped his friend, "she came to me first."

"If you two have a hotel together then I can research both of you!" Fuchsia offered.

"Dude," the one guy slurred to the other, "she's not even that drunk."

"Look, can I follow you around or not?" Fuchsia lost her patience.

"Let's get more drinks!" The second guy offered, and she agreed.

The three walked down the boardwalk and stopped at a beach bar where they could bury their feet in the sand. Asking the bartender for a "sea cocktail," unsure of what it would even consist of, the three of them sipped on a pitcher of an ocean-blue concoction.

"So what exactly is this project you're working on?" The boy asked.

"The human experience," Fuchsia replied. "Wait a minute, *I'm* the one who's supposed to be asking the questions! Gosh, you humans are so tricky!" She tilted her head and giggled.

"I told you she's on something," he nudged to his friend.

Suddenly, out of nowhere, Fuchsia was hit with a huge wave of sadness. She found herself yearning for the Captain like never before. With each sip, she felt like she could hear the call of his ship.

Fuchsia felt overcome with loneliness. Perhaps it was not actually *distraction*, but *loneliness*, that defined the human condition. But when she imagined the Captain, she never pictured loneliness. The ocean was his mistress and it was all he ever needed. He was never alone. *Was he even human? No, of course not!*

"I have to go find the Captain!" Fuchsia shot up from her chair.

"Wait!" they stopped her, "What about your project? You were about to ask questions?"

"Right," Fuchsia nodded, sitting back down and snapping out of her daze. *Jeez, being a human really is distracting,* she thought. "I was going to ask," she continued, "what does it mean to be a human? Coming from a real human being, obviously."

"Uh, that sounds like a science question," one of the boys replied, "look it up."

"Idiot," the other one said, "she got no phone!"

"Okay, chill," he pulled out his phone and read, *"to have the ability to..."*

"No, no," Fuchsia shook her head with frustration, "I told you I want to hear the answer from a *real human being*! Not a *robot!*" Perhaps not 'distraction' nor 'loneliness' defined the human condition, but 'stupidity'! She thought. "Tell me, as a real human being..." she slowed down her words, "what does it mean to be a human?"

"It means you like to drink. Can I get you another?"

Fuchsia stared at both boys blankly and paused for a moment. All hope was lost. There was too much miscommunication.

"Thank you so much for your participation, unfortunately I will have to choose new subjects to research. Goodbye and good luck," she gave them a polite smile and then walked away.

"Wait!" They called out, but Fuchsia disappeared into the crowd as fast as she could.

Something about being human was making her feel especially irritable and she had no time for beating around the bush. She just wanted to be a mermaid again. She didn't realize being human would make her feel this *heavy*. And yet, as heavy as she felt, there was still a gaping, hollow hole inside of her.

What does it mean to be a mermaid? I'll never know, and I'll never be able to go back...

In darkness, Fuchsia ran through the beach to the edge of the ocean. She dipped her toes in the water. It was ice cold this time of night, but the water felt like home. She missed having a tail, but could still admire the arch of her feet.

These feet may never let me swim those deep shores I once lived in, but they can walk me to places I have never gone before…

Fuchsia had lost hope in ever becoming a mermaid again, but perhaps this was not such a bad thing after all. There were no more mermaid secrets to keep. No more special powers to protect. There was absolutely nothing left to lose!

How uncomfortable it felt to be human. And yet, how opportunistic! She now had the whole world at her feet…

VII. A STORMY CRYSTAL BALL

T hat night, Fuchsia fell fast asleep on the sandy beach. The sound of crashing waves was soothing, compared to the silent stillness of water she was used to falling asleep to.

Upon waking up, she felt re-energized. It was time for a new adventure. Her first day had been a lot to take in, pushing herself to talk to real humans for the very first time.

She found life as a mermaid to be so dull and predictable, and yet now she was finding the human world to be tremendously over-whelming. There was so much to learn.

Fuchsia could not escape her eagerness to pursue true romance. Images of the Captain continued flooding through her head. However, it was no use -- yearning for someone who would not come to her rescue.

A part of her imagined that immersing herself in the human world would be the proof he needed to see that she was brave enough for him. Perhaps, she hoped, that after falling asleep on the sand, she would wake up magically in his arms. But that was not the case.

In absolute frustration, Fuchsia had no choice but to continue insisting to herself that he was only a dream. True love was merely a fantasy. Mermaids were meant to explore, not to be tied down. And no one, most especially the Captain, was to be trusted.

Fuchsia also had to remind herself that Mother Mermaid would never send her out into the human world if she thought she couldn't handle it. In fact, this is exactly what she had been praying for -- a challenge. After a lifetime of being told to fear the humans, she found them to be surprisingly approachable. For as long as she could keep her true mermaid identity a secret, she felt unharmed. And still, the possibility of being caught was just enough danger to keep her heart racing.

After a single day surrounded by humans, Fuchsia concurred that they weren't so evil after all. Of course they had issues, but that stemmed down to distraction, loneliness, and stupidity. Fuchsia was well aware of her naive optimism and childlike hope. She knew that her openness about the human world was somewhat questionable, just like her dream of finding true love someday. So then, she wondered, why so much distrust towards the Captain -- the man I may be in love with?

Snapping out of her daze, Fuchsia quit overthinking, and headed towards the boardwalk. Her stiff legs trembled; walking on two feet was still quite the adjustment.

Sniffing, Fuchsia felt a pang of hunger take over. Yesterday had been so adventurous that she completely forgot about her appetite. And now it was hitting her like an angry beast.

Continuing to sniff, she felt the warmth of oil traveling up her nasal passage and taking over her entire body. There was another, much more unfamiliar scent. It was very... *sweet*!

Fuchsia's nose led her to a glowing sign that read "CREPE SHOP." Below the sign was a set of several tables filled with many, many humans -- chatting, laughing, and chowing down.

Fuchsia paused, scanning the scene, wondering how she could get her hands on whatever it was they were eating.

Her heart skipped a beat when she spotted those two familiar boys from last night. They were sitting at a table with two other girls. Desperate for familiarity, she ran over to them, relieved to find someone she recognized.

"Hey!" She exclaimed with bubbly joy, "remember me?"

"Oh!" They both responded with shock.

"We thought we lost you," one of them added.

"We were just about to leave, but you can hang with us if you want," the other offered -- it was the first boy who she had met yesterday.

"That would be wonderful!" Fuchsia smiled with delight.

"Are you feeling better now?" The second boy asked.

"Well," Fuchsia sighed, "yesterday, there was a lot to take in, everything seemed so new and strange. But I think I'm starting to get the hang of things. I'm starving though! Can you help me find something to eat?"

The two girls, in silent confusion, gave the boys a strange look.

"She was on a weird drug last night," the second boy explained.

"Ohhh," the girls nodded with understanding.

"Yeah," he continued, "a bad trip."

"Nuh-uh!" Fuchsia threw her hands in the air. "I don't even know what a 'drug' is! Where I come from, we only do sea cocktails!"

"Mm-hmm," the second boy continued with a sarcastic smirk, "sure..."

"Just cut it out," the first boy nudged.

As the group stood up to get going, the first boy called out, "you guys go ahead, I'll stay here with Fuchsia so she can have some breakfast."

"Alright!" The second boy perked up, happy to be alone with the two giggly girls, who politely waved goodbye.

"You remember my name?" Fuchsia asked the first boy with surprise as the rest of the group disappeared down the boardwalk.

"Of course," he nodded without hesitance, "what kind of crepe do you want?"

"What's a crepe? And, also, what's your name?"

"I'm Zale."

"Oh," Fuchsia smiled.

"A crepe is like a thin pancake. You can add chocolate, cinnamon, banana, strawberries, sugar... anything you want," he casually shrugged.

"Okay," Fuchsia nodded.

"So, what would you like?"

"Yes!"

"Huh?"

"I'll take all of it! Whatever it is! I told you, I'm really, really hungry!" She widened her eyes and vigorously rubbed her stomach.

With an adoring chuckle, Zale took Fuchsia to the chef and ordered her an "everything" crepe. After paying, he handed Fuchsia her meal. They walked over to a wooden bench facing the ocean waves.

Totally starry-eyed, Fuchsia looked at her crepe with amazement, and then shoved it down her throat.

"Wow, you weren't kidding," he let out an amused giggle.

"Whoa, whoa, whoa!" Fuchsia screamed, "my mouth is exploding!" Her black pupils dilated enormously.

Befuddled, and a little scared, Zale was speechless and simply continued to stare.

"Where I come from, all we eat is fish! This is so much more *yummy!!!*" Fuchsia squealed like a child.

The only sweetness she had ever tasted was a sea cocktail, and that came along with a bitter aftertaste. Merpeople made their sea cocktails by taking sea water and zapping it with their magical powers, the closest thing they had to mankind's version of alcohol. Other than that, her whole diet consisted of fish, kelp, and sea plants.

"Where are you from, the Mediterranean?" Zale questioned.

"Sure, something like that," Fuchsia nodded, chewing with her mouth open.

"You know, I was surprised to see you this morning."

"Why's that?" Fuchsia asked with her mouth full, still chewing.

"Last night you just rushed off without saying goodbye. I thought I did something wrong."
"Oh..." Fuchsia slowed down, catching her breath as she finished up eating. Her stomach was feeling much better now. Finally, after a hearty swallow, she explained, "I'm sorry. Like I said, I was very overwhelmed... and..."

"Yeah?" Zale leaned in, urging for more.

After a short pause, Fuchsia admitted, "I got really nervous when I came back to the boardwalk this morning... which is weird, because I never have social anxiety. Somehow, all of a sudden I was terrified. And then as soon as I saw you, I felt this strange sense of comfort... like you were an old friend, even though we just met. And I knew you could help me out," Fuchsia paused again, and then said, "oh wow, I'm rambling! I'm sorry!"

"No, no!" Zale shook his head, "that's very sweet," he leaned in closer to her, "I'm glad you see me that way."

Fuchsia felt her face flush.

"I hope you know that those girls I was with earlier, you don't have to worry about them."

"Huh?" Fuchsia tilted her head, perplexed.

"I don't like them that way. They're just friends. It's really my man Seth who's trying to get with them. But they're not my type."

"Okay," Fuchsia nodded, beginning to feel uncomfortable.

Zale inched in even closer now, like he was thinking about kissing her.

Fuchsia slid right backwards, away from him, "can we go somewhere?" She asked, "I want some adventure!"

"Sure!" Zale eagerly nodded, "I can show you adventure!"

And so, the two got up from the bench and walked down the boardwalk together. Fuchsia looked all around, observing the silly human behavior, checking out all the quirky shops, and taking in the breathtaking scenery of the beach.

Living deep in the ocean was pretty, but everything was mainly blue, with the occasional splash of colorful coral. In contrast, being right on the edge of the water was thrilling -- the sound of waves crashing, watching them go back and forth... the way the sand sparkles in the sunlight... the fluffy white clouds subtly passing by... and most of all, the bright, shining, overpowering sun.

As exhilarating and striking as it all was, the one thing Fuchsia struggled the most with, was gravity. Feeling glued to the ground, unable to swim freely in any direction, she felt so restricted. Walking was far more draining than swimming. After several minutes of walking, Fuchsia couldn't believe that they had only traveled a few blocks -- swimming would've taken them a much further distance.

Zale was silent as Fuchsia was deep in her head, taking it all in, comparing the human world to her previous mermaid life. As she perceived her surroundings with awe, Zale was perceiving Fuchsia was awe.

"Phew," Fuchsia let out a deep breath, "I'm exhausted."

"We don't have to keep walking," Zale suggested, "we could go sit somewhere again, go to the beach... what do you wanna do?"

The two of them stopped, and Fuchsia turned her head to see a large sign that read "PSYCHIC."

"AH!" Fuchsia screeched in elation, "we must go to the psychic!"

"Whatever you want," he agreed without any resistance, following her inside like a puppy-dog.

There was something about a psychic that felt like 'home' to Fuchsia, reminding her of the merpeople, who's intuitions were significantly more developed than the human's -- who's intuitions were severely stunted. That's why humans had never been able to prove the existence of mermaids and mermen -- despite their advanced technology, their faulty intuition has always led them astray, with their lack of ability to comprehend a world of intellectual species outside of their own.

"Welcome," greeted an elder woman wearing a brown shirt with a long, indigo skirt, her whole body covered in crystal jewelry. She had many wrinkles, but wore them gracefully like lines of wisdom.

The room was small, and dimly lit with candles that smelled like vanilla and lavender. There was quiet, ambient music playing softly in the background. A surge of tranquility came upon Fuchsia.

"Hi," Fuchsia greeted back, "I'm Fuchsia."

"Nice to meet you, Fuchsia," the psychic nodded, "you can call me 'Madame.' Please, take a seat," she motioned.

Fuchsia plopped herself down on a red, velvet couch. Madame, the psychic, sat across from her in a large, golden chair resembling a throne. Between them was a table with purple cloth draped over it. On the table were several crystals, a stack of cards, and a wondrous crystal ball.

Zale stood in the corner and watched from a distance.

"Let me see your hand," Madame ordered.

As per instruction, Fuchsia reached out her right hand and let Madame take a look.

"Hmm," Madame muttered, intentently focused. She touched the webs in between Fuchsia's fingers, noticing how prompt they were. "You're a mermaid," she calmly concluded.

Fuchsia widened her eyes as her heart sank, and then quickly turned to Zale to see his reaction.

"Yes," Zale agreed, still standing far off in the corner with his arms crossed, "beautiful and magical, just like a mermaid."

Fuchsia felt so exposed, but luckily Zale was completely oblivious. Madame seemed otherworldly, like she knew all about the mermaid world, but would never spill their secrets. She felt a comforting sense of trust from this unknown woman.

"Madame," Fuchsia gulped, "I must ask... can you tell me anything about... the Captain?" She clenched her jaw with anxiety.

"Let me consult my crystal ball," Madame said, pulling it towards her and looking deep into the clear glass, cupping her hands around it.

Zale was in absolute disbelief when he saw actual figures moving around inside the crystal ball, playing out like a movie, "whoa!" he shouted, "is that CGI or something? How'd you do that?" he came a bit closer, glaring deeply at the crystal with skepticism.

"Aha!" The psychic exclaimed, "I see your future!"

"What do you see?" Fuchsia implored with urgency.

"I see you and the Captain, together forever."

Gasping, Fuchsia questioned, "really!?"

"Yes, husband and wife."

"What else?" Fuchsia was incredibly anxious for more.

"I see babies. Lots and lots of babies."

"How many!?"

"I see the two of you surrounded by... ten kids, to be exact!"

"Oh my goodness!" Fuchsia squawked with joy. "Where is the Captain right now?"

Madame paused, her expression suddenly shifted from dazzlement to reluctance.

"What is it?" Fuchsia ground her teeth in consternation.

"Oh, dear..."

"What!?"

The crystal ball turned dark and cloudy. There were lightning strikes and sounds of thunder.

"Wh-why is it all stormy?" Fuchsia's entire body filled up with dread.

"I am now looking into the present," Madame explained.

"Do you see the Captain? Where is he?"

"He has a girlfriend… no, he has many girlfriends…"

"He does?"

"But none of them are mermaids."

"Oh," Fuchsia felt slightly relieved, yet still terribly concerned.

"He has a message for you."

"He does?" Fuchsia perked up.

"He wants you to know that he's having lots of fun."

Fuchsia deflated back down in her seat, "well, why would he want to tell me *that?*" she whimpered.

"I see that you two can have a beautiful future together. However, only if you choose it."

"What does that mean? This is my destiny, isn't it?"

"Only if you want it to be. You have a marvelous destiny awaiting you, but as I said, only if you choose it."

"I don't understand," Fuchsia sighed in frustration, "choose my destiny? Isn't that the whole point of destiny, you *can't* choose it?"

"Of course you can! You are far more powerful than you give yourself credit for!"

"Then what's the point of destiny, if it might not even happen?" Fuchsia whined.

"Destiny is a gift reserved for the brave. The universe hands you a golden opportunity, and it's your choice whether you decide to reach out and take it or not. And the one thing that determines your choice is bravery."

"Aha..." Fuchsia thought deeply, trying to fully grasp the message, "so, what you're saying is... the Captain is my destiny... but only if I am brave enough for him?"

"I'm saying that, if a future with the Captain, with ten kids and a happily ever after, is what your heart desires, then you shall receive... but first, you must work for it."

"Work for it?"

"If someone is meant for you, they come to you effortlessly... but if you're blinded by fear, then you'll never realize that they have been standing right in front of you all along..." Madame briefly glanced at Zale, "and so you have to work through those fears, if you ever want to be together."

"I think I'm starting to get it," Fuchsia enthused, "please, go on!"

"If you would let go of your fears, you would see clearly that the Captain is much closer than you think..." Madame winked.

"That's enough!" Zale cut in with anger, "how much are you charging for this nonsense, anyway?"

"No, wait!" Fuchsia panicked, "please, tell me more, Madame! You have to help me!"

"I'm afraid we've reached the end of our session," Madame announced, "that'll be one-hundred dollars."

"But I don't have any money!" Fuchsia cried out, turning to Zale with puppy-dog eyes.

"You have got to be effing kidding me," Zale muttered under his breath, and then with a heavy sigh, handed Madame a credit card from his wallet.

"We can continue for two-hundred," Madame offered.

"No way," Zale furiously shook his head, "c'mon, Fuchsia, let's go."

With disappointment, Fuchsia stood up from the velvet couch and grudgingly let herself out the door. Before exiting, she turned back to Madame and said, "thank you Madame, that was very helpful."

"Anytime," Madame smiled, "and please, do come back."

"I will."

VIII. UNAPOLOGETIC EMOTIONS

& Radical Self-Acceptance

Returning to the crowded boardwalk, Fuchsia pulled out a shiny, little penny from her pocket that she had found earlier. She handed it to Zale.

"Here, a token of my appreciation. I'm not sure how much one-hundred dollars is, but surely this coin is worth more than a piece of plastic."

"Good one," he rolled his eyes.

"I think I better go now," Fuchsia told him.

"Wait!" He grabbed her shoulder with urgency, "tell me, who is this Captain guy?"

Taken aback by his demanding energy, Fuchsia simply responded, "he's my destiny."

"Now, why's that? Just sounds like a player to me..."

Fuchsia felt uncomfortable standing in the middle of the board-walk with everyone rushing by, so she asked, "can we go some-where quiet real fast?"

"Definitely!" Zale nodded, leading her around the corner to a grassy field.

They found another bench to sit on, a marble one, facing a small fountain with little birds flying about. There were still many people, but much further away now.

"What's on your mind?" he asked.

"My intuition is a bit weaker than normal, but I can still *see...*"

"See what?"

"I can still see that, well, to be frank, you've got a thing for me!" Fuchsia chuckled with awkwardness.

Zale's face went red, "oh, do I?"

"And to be even more blunt, you're not the first... or the last... in fact, it seems that every guy I meet falls hard for me."

Zale laughed uncomfortably, "is that so?"

"I don't wanna sound conceited or anything... but it's true! It happens all the time!"

"Well, you're a very beautiful girl. I wouldn't doubt that."

"Which is why I better be going. The Captain would be furious if he saw us together."

"He'd be jealous, huh?" Zale smirked with cockiness.

"Uh... I guess so, yeah," Fuchsia hesitated.

"So you're not into me?"

"I mean, I like you as a friend."

"A boyfriend?"

"No, I said *friend*," she rolled her eyes, becoming annoyed.

"A boy who's a friend. What's the difference?"

"There's a *huge* difference!" Fuchsia threw her arms up.

"Tell me," he smirked again.

"Ugh," Fuchsia scoffed, "a boyfriend is someone you have a romantic connection with. A friend is just a friend. Duh!"

"Don't you feel connections with your friends? Isn't that what a friend is?"

Fuchsia wouldn't give up her argument, "it's platonic, not romantic!"

"Don't you love your friends?"

"Yes, but in a different way!"

"Tell me the difference," he grinned.

"Okay," Fuchsia growled, with persistence, refusing to back down, "with a boyfriend, it's physical... you wanna touch, you wanna kiss, you wanna..." she waited for a second... "make love."

A very wide smile spread across Zale's face, "that's exactly what I wanna do," he blushed, "that would make me your boyfriend."

"It has to be *mutual!*" Fuchsia nearly shouted across the field, giving his shoulder a gentle shove. "You're just teasing me at this point."

"I'm not," he said in total seriousness, "girls and boys who are friends, they're boyfriend and girlfriend. It's different from marriage. You can have a bunch of boyfriends or girlfriends, you can be on different pages, but there's a connection there. It doesn't have to be physical, but emotionally, it's there. Maybe it will progress into marriage someday or maybe it won't. So, if we're friends, then I see you as my girlfriend, the same way you call your friends who are girls, girlfriends." He caught his breath.

Fuchsia paused for a moment to think back on her own experience. She wondered, all those mermen she knew -- Marino, Finn, Reef, Gill, Oceanus, Archer, and others -- were all of them her boyfriends? Did they all see her as their girlfriend? Was it actually possible that she had been guilty of being a "player" herself? Now the line between "friend" and "girlfriend" or "boyfriend" seemed so much blurrier...

Finally, raising an eyebrow, Fuchsia asked, "so, how many girlfriends do you have then?"

"I have a lot. Those girls you saw earlier, they're my girlfriends. But that doesn't mean I want to marry them."

"Do you *like* them?"

"If I don't like someone, then they're not my friend."

"I mean... do you have a crush on them?"

"Nope. They're just my girlfriends."

"Oh, you just say that for the ego trip!" Fuchsia pushed him once again.

"You sound jealous," he taunted, pushing her back this time.

"So, you haven't kissed them or anything?"

"No, I haven't," he leaned in close, like he was doing earlier in the day, like he was still thinking about kissing her.

Fuchsia felt a fiercely strong heat. She couldn't deny that there was a connection there. But nevertheless, he wasn't the Captain. She failed to comprehend why, but the Captain was all she could think about, even though it seemed they hardly even knew each other. The closer she got to Zale, the more she ached in pain, yearning for the Captain's arms.

"Zale," she stopped him from leaning in any further, "my heart is with someone else."

"I see," he backed off, finally admitting defeat.

"You better go catch up with your friends."

"I'll go," he reassured, "are you going to be okay, though? You weren't serious last night about sleeping on the sand, right? You have a place to stay? Your family's around?" He was terribly concerned.

"I'll be fine on my own."

"If you change your mind or you need a place to sleep, I'm staying at the Sea Salt hotel, room 207, on the second floor. It's on Neptune Road, right by the center of town."

"Alright."

"I'm here all summer, so hopefully we run into each other again."

Fuchsia silently nodded and watched him stand up and start to walk away. She felt awful; he was a kind boy with a seemingly genuine heart. He deserved a great love.

"Zale!" She called out, "have fun with your girlfriends!"

"Oh, I'm having lots of fun," he giggled.

"And your boyfriend, too!" Fuchsia added with a laugh.

Zale waved and continued on his way.

Completely alone, once again, Fuchsia let out a deep sigh. She missed the Captain so badly, she needed to find a way to see him. But there was no way she could swim back to that rock with her faulty human legs. Plus, she didn't even know her directions, or how to get back there.

Fuchsia started missing her sisters now, too. Only about twenty four hours now since she left the mermaid world behind, and it all seemed like a distant dream. She questioned her true intentions to leave it all behind in the first place -- to find something more, or to find the Captain? Or both?

"Mother Mermaid?" Fuchsia discreetly whispered to herself in prayer, "remind me again: why am I here?"

A moment of silence.

Fuchsia remembered now -- because life as a mermaid was so dull and boring, so safe and sheltered, so predictable... and she was craving a challenge. But, she wondered, what type of challenge am I looking for? What am I trying to gain?

She could not escape it -- her desire to be in love. Not the type of love that mermaids were accustomed to: dating all types of mermen left and right, kissing them all, free to be with whoever. She wanted a strong and passionate romance, the type where two souls are conjoined for eternity, and no one else can stand in their way. She wanted an anchor, someone to tie her down, someone to dedicate her entire life to. Although her sisters often teased her about her narcissistic tendencies and inflated confidence, Fuchsia never wanted to live for herself, but for someone else...

Perhaps, Fuchsia pondered, it was time to give up on the Captain. There was no way of finding him at this point. Even though Madame saw him in her destiny, at this moment, he was nowhere to be found. Maybe she needed to let him find her.

Yet, as she was told by Madame, if she wanted to let him find her, she would first have to work through her fears. And what better place to work through your fears, than the terrifying world of distracted, lonely, and stupid human beings?!

It was time to venture further into the human world, time to meet more people, time to find more adventure. Through her hardships, she would grow stronger, and finally feel brave enough to face her Captain.

The day she met the Captain and he invited her on his ship, she denied him because of fear. All those days she spent on that rock in the middle of the sea, watching the Captain sail by and never saying a word, only staring at him in awe and praying for him to come closer -- it was fear that was stopping them from being together. And when she finally decided to run towards him, but she saw him with another woman, she once again let fear get in the way. She knew their passion was otherworldly, strong enough to overcome any "girlfriend" of his. Looking back, there were countless opportunities to have their happily ever after. If only she hadn't been so full of fear!

Fuchsia was confident that a bit more time in the human world would give her the faith she needed. And this time, when the Captain came back for her, she would be ready.

Just then, a small family passed by. There was a man and a woman, the man pushing a stroller with a baby, and the woman rubbing her pregnant belly. That's when Fuchsia knew -- she wanted to be a mother. The desire hit her like a strike of lightning.

Fuchsia marched as fast as she could back to the psychic, to speak with Madame.

"Back so soon!" Madame cheered.

Hastily scanning the room, to make sure no other customers were there, Fuchsia saw that it was safe -- just Madame and her.

"I don't have any money," Fuchsia confessed, "but... I need more answers!"

"I'm sorry," Madame replied, "this is a business -- no money, no service."

Money was such a strange concept for Fuchsia. Back in the ocean, all she needed was her charisma to get what she wanted.

Presumptuously plopping herself back on the velvet couch, Fuchsia discreetly leaned in and quietly whispered, "how did you know that I'm a mermaid?"

Appalled, Madame answered, "darling, mermaid or not, rules are rules -- no money, no service!"

"Have you had other mermaids come to you before?" Fuchsia could hardly contain herself, "and why did you keep looking at Zale like that? Do you think he could secretly be a merman?"

"Honey, I'd love to do another, far more in-depth reading on you. But I'm going to continue repeating myself -- lady's gotta pay the bills!"

"But, I need help!" Fuchsia pouted, "c'mon, from one intuitive woman to another."

"Darling, how do I say this kindly? You're not special. Customers are equal in my eyes. Beg and plead all you want, but I won't make an exception for the girl who's always used to getting her way."

Raising her eyebrows, Fuchsia was shocked by Madame's abruptness -- yet also disturbingly aware of how she was overstepping Madame's boundaries. There was a pang in her heart.
And so, she gracefully stood up and made her way out the door -- but not before turning back and adding, "you know, I'm a famous actress, where I come from. I used to have pink hair. I used to be breathtaking. And now I'm brokenhearted, lost and alone."

Fuchsia's fury grew more powerful, "You're wrong! I'm not like all customers -- I'm practically an alien! This isn't my home! You know how many times I stuck up for the human race? How often I asked my fellow merpeople -- why can't we help the humans? And they were right, because you're all selfish! You don't care about helping one another, all you care about is money! All I'm asking is that you answer a few questions!" Her face turned red.

Madame sighed a heavy sigh, as Fuchsia stood there angrily in the doorway, awaiting her response.

"Take care, now," Madame calmly told her.

In exasperation, Fuchsia left the psychic shop in a huff.

Spotting a shaded garden area for her to cool down in, Fuchsia sat on the grass and took a few deep breaths. It was fully hitting her now -- her safe and spoiled mermaid world was no longer. This was the human world, and it was harsh. This was the only way she could grow.

Fuchsia took a few deep breaths. In and out. Inhale, exhale...

"All of the answers you seek are within," she could hear Mother Mermaid distantly purring to her.

Looking around in total confusion, she had no idea how she had gotten here. Stuck inside her head, Fuchsia attempted to piece it all together. She recalled how unhappy she was in her mermaid world, because there was so much pressure to be happy all the time. Here in the human world, she saw so many children crying, and so many adults yelling and screaming. It was actually refreshing.

Earlier, she had observed a little boy who refused to eat his dinner. His mother was yelling at him, and in return, he cried and screamed, causing the mother to yell back even louder. It was ironically endearing.

Along the beach, by the crashing waves, there were so many screams and shrieks. There was a boy who collected a bucket full of ocean water and poured it on top of an unsuspecting girl who was trying to take a nap on the sand. In return, she screeched at the top of her lungs, chased him down and threw him into the sand. It was hysterical.

There were so many people yelling, screaming, and shrieking -- running away from each other, chasing after one another -- it was madness. And for some odd reason, Fuchsia liked that madness.

It struck her to think that she had just shouted at a total stranger in such a disrespectful tone. It was so *"un-mermaid"* of her to do! Normally, the only safe space for her to be emotional was in her scripted plays. But acting out in real life was a completely different type of rush. It was invigorating, it was bold, it was passionate.

Being surrounded by all the chaos of the humans in this little beach town, Fuchsia was sort of, ever so slightly, feeling at home. The ocean world was too quiet and peaceful. The human world was a constant war -- which somehow felt more freeing. Everyone here was so unapologetically emotional, and Fuchsia loved it.

Fuchsia proudly whispered to herself with radical acceptance, "I am emotional!" And just as she said this, a swarm of birds flew above her. She looked up at them in amazement.

Fuchsia considered rushing back to the psychic to apologize to Madame for her humiliating outburst -- but then again, she wondered, *why?* For, she wasn't sorry for revealing her genuine frustration. She meant every word she had spoken. So, she decided, she would not apologize. She was proud of her anger. It was brave.

IX. THE LONELY MERMAID

Fuchsia spent the rest of the evening sitting on a boardwalk bench, continuing to study human behavior. She was on the lookout for another friend group she could join, like Zale's, but no one else had the same welcoming energy.

Fuchsia said "hi" to multiple passersby, but only some of them greeted her back, and all of them kept on walking forward.

"Can I hang out with you guys?" Fuchsia blurted out in desperation to a group of people who looked about her age.

"Um," they all hesitated, "we're just on our way home, sorry!" A girl said.

Fuchsia nodded with disappointment, and then watched them walk into a restaurant. Surely, that couldn't be where they live, Fuchsia determined.

Another group of friends came by -- "hey, can I follow you guys?" Fuchsia asked. One boy quickly glanced at her while the rest avoided eye contact and kept on moving.

"Jeez, humans are kind of mean," Fuchsia muttered to herself in embarrassment.

In the ocean, all the merpeople were always trying to hang out and talk with her, most especially the mermen. No one would ever leave her alone. And now, these humans were walking right through her like thin air. She wondered, was it because her hair was boring-brown now, instead of her usual show-stopping-pink? Was it because she had lost all her mermaid magic?

Again, another group came by, and Fuchsia continued trying.

Waving her arms around for attention, Fuchsia said to them, "can I join you guys?"

They all stopped.

"Aww!" A woman exclaimed, "are you lost, little girl?"

"No, just homeless," Fuchsia explained.

"Oh my goodness, you poor thing!" She shrieked, "do you have any money for food?"

"I've been finding some pennies."

"Oh, let me buy you some dinner!"

"That would be wonderful! I'm starving!" Fuchsia lit up, her stomach grumbling.

"I'll be right back!"

Sure enough, the group disappeared, but the woman returned with a burger and fries.

"Here!" She handed her the meal. The woman had a buzz cut with tons of piercings and tattoos. She looked like a living piece of art -- it was beautiful.

"Wow, thank you!" Fuchsia said with graciousness.

Perhaps she had judged humans too harshly. After being ignored by so many, finally she found someone who was kind.

"Of course, sweetie," she said, "what happened, did you get kicked out?"

"Sort of," Fuchsia answered -- of course, she would have to leave out the details that it was technically the great goddess, Mother Mermaid, who kicked her out of the ocean.

"Is there anyone you can stay with tonight? A friend, or any family?"

"I was thinking of sleeping on the sand again."

She gasped, "oh, no! Sure, there has to be someone you can stay with. Don't you have any friends nearby? Do you need a lift?"

"Well," Fuchsia considered, "I do have one friend. He's staying at the Sea Salt hotel."

"Oh, that's just a few blocks away! Totally walking distance! Do you need directions? I can help you find it!"

"That's okay," Fuchsia shook her head, "I was actually just looking for someone I could hang out with, get to know..."

"Oh honey, you should really go find your friend immediately, it's getting dark soon. You don't wanna be out here all alone, it's super dangerous. There's tons of creeps around, it's not safe.

Please, go find your friend!"

Disappointed, Fuchsia tried to explain, "I'm not looking for safety, I'm looking for adventure! Could I join you and your friends? I'm sure you all would like me! I'm tremendously entertaining!"

The woman laughed, "I'm sure you're a lot of fun. But seriously, you need to be smart and go find that friend of yours. My friends and I are about to get plastered, and it'd be terribly irresponsible of me to have you join us. But I'll tell you what, if you and your friend want to come join us later, you're totally welcome. I just don't like to see a young girl like you all alone, especially in a vulnerable situation like this. I've been there before."

"If you insist," Fuchsia nodded in defeat, seeing that this woman was massively disturbed.

"I'm Shayla, by the way."

"I'm Fuchsia."

"So nice to meet you, Fuchsia. Promise me you'll find that friend and be safe?"

"Promise," Fuchsia felt obligated to say.

"My parents kicked me out of the house at your age for telling them I was gay. You're not alone, okay? You still have love and support."

"Thank you," Fuchsia smiled as they parted ways, and she had no choice but to head down the boardwalk. She had been told her whole life by fellow merpeople that the human world was scary and unsafe, but to hear those words from the mouth of an actual human was chilling.

As the sun continued to set, Fuchsia's fears began to heighten. She assumed that embarking on this daunting journey would allow her to conquer her fears, but they were only growing worse. The more time she spent around humans, the more rejected she felt. And now she could see that Zale was truly a rare gem, for being the only human willing to give her a chance. After promising a stranger she'd go find him, she pondered whether she actually should or not. His energy was unlike anyone else's. Nonetheless, even if the Captain really did have many girlfriends, the thought of going back to Zale felt wrong.

Fuchsia continued walking down the boardwalk, lost in her thoughts, now reaching a sidewalk, continuing with her head in the clouds, when seemingly out of nowhere, the Sea Salt Hotel appeared right in front of her.

"Room 207, second floor," she thought out loud, remembering Zale's words.

She stood still for a minute, facing the hotel. There was a sinking feeling in her stomach. She couldn't do it. Instead, she ran back towards the beach. Finding a soft spot in the sand, she let herself rest.

Shayla -- the woman she had just met earlier -- her voice was running through her head, telling her how dangerous it was to be alone at night as a young girl. The first night she had fallen asleep on the sand so peacefully, trusting that Mother Mermaid was protecting her, but now she wasn't so sure.

"I could get kidnapped by a pirate!" Fuchsia kept fearing. "I could get washed away by the ocean, and not be able to breathe or swim, now that I'm human! I could get assaulted, or murdered!"

"AHHH!" Fuchsia uncontrollably screamed at the top of her

lungs. She had never been more scared before in her life.

Running away from the beach, she found herself right back at the Sea Salt Hotel. There she was, bouncing between two fears -- being vulnerably alone, versus being vulnerable with another person. Taking a deep breath, she turned off her thoughts, and rushed right inside.

Heading straight towards the stairs, she was stopped by a woman behind a large desk.

"Excuse me, are you checking in?" she inquired.

"I'm here to see Zale," Fuchsia explained, "I'm, uh… a girlfriend of his!"

"Hmm," she nodded, looking at her computer, "do you know the room number?"

"207, second floor!"

"Very well," she said, dismissing Fuchsia.

With a shrug, Fuchsia continued her venture up the stairs. Her heart pounded when she found herself in front of the room numbered "207." Feeling a pulse throughout her body, she went ahead and knocked three times.

Merely a few seconds later, the door swung wide open -- and there was Zale, looking like a puppy-dog greeting its owner who'd left him at home all day.

"Fuchsia!" he nearly cried out.

"Hi," she slightly grinned.

"Come in," he said as she walked inside. "So, you changed your mind."

"Don't get all cocky, now," Fuchsia rolled her eyes, "I just got rejected by every single person on the boardwalk, that doesn't make you special or anything."

"Alright," he nodded in slight confusion.

"Apparently sleeping on the beach is hazardous or something, so, I suppose this would be the more ideal option."

"You don't have to explain anything. Don't tell me why you came here. I have a spare bed, so don't worry, I'm not gonna try kissing you or anything creepy like that," he put his hands up in defense.

"Good," Fuchsia quickly nodded, then plopped herself on the bed with exhaustion, "I am *soooo* tired!"

"It's only eight o'clock."

"And your point is...? By the way, it's totally strange that you randomly have this spare bed here. Is this reserved for all your girlfriends? And where are they, anyway? And where's your boyfriend?"

"My friends went out for dinner and drinks. I left after dinner. My stomach felt weird."

"Yeah, my stomach hurts, too," Fuchsia rubbed her belly, "I think it's from eating all this new food."

"Yeah, boardwalk food is pretty greasy," Zale shrugged.

"I have to say, it's hard to believe we just met. You feel like an old friend."

"And how long have you known this Captain guy?"

"The Captain? It's been about a year or so, although we've only had one conversation."

"You're kidding me."

"What?"

"One conversation!?" Zale's jaw dropped, "and you're madly in love with him?"

"It was love at first sight. You wouldn't understand."

"Oh, I know love at first sight," he stared deep into Fuchsia's eyes.

"Are you in love with me?" she joked.

Zale blushed, speechless.

"You're in love with me!" Fuchsia shot up from the bed and bursted with joy, "I put a spell on you, huh?"

"I didn't say anything," Zale turned his head.

"You're sweet," Fuchsia giggled, falling back onto the bed.

"I think the only reason you're so obsessed with this Captain guy is because he's unattainable. If he was standing right in front of you, telling you he's in love, you'd just laugh. I think you're in love with a dream."

"Excuse me?" Fuchsia, once again, shot back upward. She furrowed her eyebrows in disgust, "who do you think you are? First of all, stop saying 'Captain guy,' it's 'thee Captain,' with a capital

'C'!'" Her anger was strengthening, "and secondly, he *did* tell me he loved me! And I... I... wait..." Fuchsia paused, lowering her voice, "did I really laugh at him when he told me he was in love with me?"

"Hmm?" Zale crossed his arms.

"Uh, oh," Fuchsia slammed her palm to her head, "that wasn't very nice of me, was it?"

Zale remained silent.

"But what he did to me was ten times worse! Listen, he sailed right past me every day. I kept waiting for him to come closer. And then, finally, he sends me a letter promising he'll be at the Mermaid Ball... and never shows!" Fuchsia instantly covered her mouth in regret. She got so caught up in her emotions that she completely forgot about covering her mermaid identity.

But that didn't seem to phase Zale, as he replied, "Mermaid Ball? What, like a party where everyone dresses up as a mermaid?"

"Yes!" Fuchsia instantly nodded with vigor, "it's a dress-up party, you know, play-pretend! Not like *real* mermaids or anything..." she awkwardly chuckled.

"So, he invited you out and then stood you up?"

"Yeah!"

"What a jerk! That's exactly why you need to let him go!"

"Oh, but you don't understand," Fuchsia shook her head with pity, "I hurt him badly. The day we met, he said he was in love with me and invited me on his ship. And I just laughed in his face. And then I told him he was crazy, that he had hallucinated the whole thing. And then I continued going on dates with Marino, talking to Finn and Gill, even Archer was making moves on me."

"Sounds like a lot of guys."

"But then I kept seeing all these random girls with the Captain on his ship. The black-haired girl, the red-haired girl... and he didn't even care! He *wanted* me to see him with them."

"Ugh, what a loser."

"Although I think he was simply trying to make me jealous... which is sweet, right?"

"No, it's hurtful and immature."

"Yeah, you're right! And he acted like he wanted me to chase after him, but he's the man, he's supposed to do the chasing, right?"

"Sure!"

"I mean, it takes two to tango though..."

"Stop," Zale demanded, "you could go back and forth all night. It sounds to me like you're very, very confused."

Fuchsia sighed, "I'm so lost."

"Don't overthink."

"I have a tendency to do that," Fuchsia clenched.

"Let's just call it an early night. Tomorrow's a new day. I'll put on some TV and we can just relax, pass out, and tomorrow morning

I'll take you out for more crepes. Sound good?"

"Yeah," Fuchsia agreed, "what do you mean by 'TV'?"

"The television?" Zale tilted his head, "you know, the little screen that plays shows?" He joked.

Clicking the remote, Fuchsia's eyes widened.

"Whoa!" She screamed, "everything is moving so fast!"

Zale laughed with awkwardness, "you know, you can use the bathroom to change into pajamas."

"All I have is this white dress!"

"Here," Zale threw her a large t-shirt of his.

"Thanks!" Fuchsia excused herself to the bathroom and used the potty after changing. Toilets were perhaps one of the strangest phenomenons of the human world that she still struggled with, but now she found 'televisions' to be just as weird. Humans were such peculiar creatures, she concluded.

Laying in bed, as she was trying to fall asleep, Fuchsia's thoughts ran heavy. She thought of Shayla, the kind stranger who talked to her on the boardwalk, and how concerned she seemed for her. Fuchsia wanted to ask Zale -- "is it true: are humans truly scared of their own species?" But she couldn't ask that without blowing her cover as a mermaid.

Stuck in her head, she thought about how mermaids and mermen generally trust each other -- that when she sees them, she knows they're on her team, she knows that they're cheering her on. Meanwhile, humans are telling other humans to take cover and be safe, because they know how dangerous life on land is.

Lifting her head slightly to peek at Zale, in the other bed across the room, she observed that he seemed to already be fast asleep. He was quite still, almost lifeless, laying there in total peace.

For any chance that he may have been still awake, Fuchsia figured it was worth a shot to whisper, "Zale?"

Immediately opening his eyes, he responded softly with a simple, "yeah?"

"Is it normal for people to be scared of each other?"

Instantly perking up even more now, Zale lifted himself into sitting-position as Fuchsia did the same, and then answered with, "you're scared of me?"

"No!" Fuchsia giggled, although he wasn't wrong, but she continued, "like, would you say the human race is bad? As in, like, unsafe?" She struggled to come up with the right words, yet hoped Zale would understand her nonetheless.

"I think most people mean well. There's really only a miniscule amount of people who purposely do harm, people you genuinely need to distrust. But, you know what they say, a few drops of poison taints the whole pond. So, it's smart to keep your guard up, to a point."

"That makes sense," she nodded with satisfaction. "There's just a few bad apples. It's a shame they ruin it for everyone else -- otherwise there wouldn't be so much fear in the world."

"What makes you ask such a question?"

"My thoughts always run wild right as I'm trying to fall asleep."

"Yeah, me too!" He excitedly agreed, like he was happy to know he wasn't alone.

"You know," she admitted, "maybe I *am* a little scared of you..." and then proceeded to fall back into bed and coyly cover her face with the blanket.

"Oh, Fuchsia," he shook his head, "you're safe with me. If only you'd realize that."

Fuchsia remained silent, hiding under her blanket. And now it was hitting her, that she'd never been so scared in her life... especially of someone so kind.

Zale added, "it's okay, I'm shy too. You'd be surprised."

"I am *not* shy!" Fuchsia bursted out, throwing off the blanket, "I'm an actress! Back home, I put on one-woman-shows on a weekly basis, in front of my entire town!"

"You have to put on a show for me sometime," he smiled.

"Maybe," she rolled her eyes.

"It's easy to be outgoing when you're wearing a mask, or when you're pretending to be someone you're not."

"Well, you seem pretty outgoing to me... are you wearing a mask?"

"Maybe," he smirked.

"Whatever," Fuchsia rolled her eyes, "I'm going to sleep now."

"Hey, you're the one who woke me up just now," Zale teased.

"Goodnight, smart-ass!" She giggled, once again hiding back under the covers.

Zale paused for a long moment before quietly uttering to himself, "it's funny -- the world is full of sociopaths, but the ones we fear the most are the ones who we deeply love." And with that, he shut his eyes, wondering if Fuchsia had heard him -- and she did.

X. KNOCKED OVER
BY THE WAVES

After a long night's rest, Fuchsia woke up peacefully in her warm and cozy bed. It was just what she needed to soothe those achy, human legs of hers.

"Good morning," Zale greeted, already awake and dressed.

Groggily rubbing her eyes, Fuchsia greeted him back, emerging from a pile of blankets.

"Wow, your hair!" He noticed, wide-eyed.

"What *about* my hair?" Fuchsia defended, becoming self-conscious, "it's messy?"

"No! The color... it looks more... vibrant."

"More vibrant?"

"Yeah, it was sorta greyish when we first met. Now it looks more brown, almost blonde."

"Oh," Fuchsia half-smiled, "must be from the sun, or something."

"Shall we get some breakfast?"

"Mmm, yeah," Fuchsia excitedly nodded, "I'll put my dress back on," she added, excusing herself to the bathroom.

"You don't have any other spare clothes?" Zale asked from behind the closed door.

"No," Fuchsia answered, "I, uh…" she tried to come up with an excuse, but her mind had gone blank.

"You don't have to explain," Zale assured, "we can stop at one of those stores on the way, or afterwards if you prefer."

"Don't I need money for clothes?" Fuchsia understood by now that everything in the human world came with a price.

"Let me pay for you," he offered.

Fully dressed, stepping out of the bathroom, Fuchsia responded, "you can't be paying for *everything*."

"Sure I can, if you let me," he warmly smiled.

"Is that what boyfriends do?"

"Only the nice ones, when they really like a girl."

"Hmm," Fuchsia muttered with skepticism.

Fuchsia and Zale headed down the boardwalk, back to the crepe shop. Once again, he ordered crepes for the both of them and they sat down to eat. The two were silent as they both scarfed down their meals.

Finally, Fuchsia spoke, "so, what happened to your friends?"

"Guess they were out late last night," he shrugged, "probably still asleep."

"You're all staying here for the summer?"

"Yep. Sea Salt Hotel is like the party hotel here, all the young people rent out rooms for the summer; I'm here as a lifeguard but I'm off this weekend. So that's how I know them, we all work together."

"A lifeguard, huh?" Fuchsia gushed, "you rescue people?"

"You could say that, sure," he humbly replied, "or just sit on a highchair all day and blow my whistle at kids who swim too close to the rocks."

"That's cool... like a guardian angel."

"Never thought of it that way, but sure," he smirked while blushing.

Fuchsia tried to stay focused on the conversation, yet her mind continued gravitating towards the Captain. Images of him sailing past her with his manly chest pointed upwards continued cycling through her head. She kept wondering where he was, and whether he missed her or not.

The first day they met was haunting her most. She could still feel the gentle softness of his lips, the strength of his arms, the closeness of his body...

Being with Zale felt... wrong. There was no other way to describe it.

As they finished up their meal, Fuchsia sighed, "I think we should part ways now."

"Running away from me again?" He teased, "you're gonna miss out on the shopping spree. I meant it when I told you I'd pay."

"No... I shouldn't," Fuchsia hesitated.

"You know, you can't get too far in the human world without money. You're gonna need some of that."

"The *human world*?" Fuchsia's heart raced. She panicked, was he starting to catch on?

Zale froze for a moment.

Fuchsia continued, "I'll get myself a job, and then I'll have money!"

"I can help you get a lifeguard job. You'd love it, sitting on the beach all day."

"No, no," Fuchsia refused, "I'll find one myself."

"You're welcome to stay at the hotel with me, free of charge," he offered.

"No," she once again refused, "I'll figure something out."

"You are very independent," he determined, "stubbornly independent, if I may add."

Getting up from the table, Fuchsia thanked Zale for breakfast, "this was very kind of you."

"It's nothing."

"But I need to let you go now."

"If you insist, I'm not going to stop you."

"Goodbye, Zale."

"You know where I'll be."

Fuchsia nodded, and went on her way. Heading down the boardwalk on her own, she could feel Zale's eyes on her. She couldn't help but wonder if she was pushing away a great guy. Now she was beginning to question if she really was in love with the Captain, or simply the idea of him.

"Where are you, my Captain?" Fuchsia whimpered to herself in agony, "why haven't you come to my rescue, yet?"

It was time for her to prove herself, she decided. Leaning on Zale would be far too easy; she'd never work through her fears that way. Instead, she would find a job, a place to live, and earn enough money to create her own new life as a human. Surely it couldn't be that hard, right?

Walking down the boardwalk, she examined all the shops. Knowing absolutely nothing about the human culinary arts, working at a restaurant or food place was out of the question. There were gift shops, surfboard stores, bicycle rentals, and clothing boutiques... all of it was so overwhelming.

Fuchsia perked up when she found a store called "Sandy's Seashells." It was full of rocks, gemstones, crystals, and of course... seashells! The whole place reminded her of home.

In the corner of her eye, she noticed a hermit crab walking around in a small cage. Its shell was pink, just like the color her hair used to be.

"Oh, what a cute, little thing you are!" She squealed, squatting over with her hands on her knees, observing the hermit crab in delight.

"Can I help you?" A woman's voice came seemingly out of nowhere.

Fuchsia jumped up, surprised to see the sales clerk standing right next to her. She was so infatuated by the teeny creature that she nearly lost awareness of her surroundings.

"Sorry," Fuchsia went red-faced, "I absolutely adore hermit crabs."

"No need to apologize! Are you interested in buying it?"

"Wait..." Fuchsia paused, "you can *buy* animals? And then *own* them?"

"Yes, we sell hermit crabs here, along with caging and feed."

Fuchsia stood still, bitterly swallowing the concept of selling and buying animals. Not only did cooked food and manmade products come with a price, but even free-roaming animals. Suddenly a nightmare flashed through her head -- mermaids and mermen, caged in boxes, being sold to other humans to own as their slaves. Her eyes bugged out, nearly popping out of her head.

"So, are you interested?" The clerk continued.

"Uh," Fuchsia quickly snapped out of her daze, pressured to keep her cool, "I'm afraid I can't afford it. Actually, I'm looking for a job! Can I work here?"

"Unfortunately, we aren't hiring right now."

"Oh," Fuchsia bowed her head, displeased.

"Perhaps next summer," she politely forced a smile.

"Would you be able to help me at all? Any advice? I really need some money..." Suddenly, Fuchsia felt enormously discouraged.

"I'm sure someone is hiring, keep on looking around," she sympathized, observing Fuchsia's pout, "maybe I can give my boss your resume, just in case."

"Resume...?" Fuchsia asked, befuddled.

"Yes, you know, a list of all your previous jobs and education."

"I don't... have any of that..." Fuchsia shyly revealed with embarrassment.

"Why don't you give me your contact information, then. What's your phone number?"

"I... I don't... have a phone," she practically whispered in shame.

"Oh, I see," she awkwardly nodded.

"Excuse me," Fuchsia quickly ran off before the clerk could even respond.

Tears streamed down her cheeks. She had never felt so dumb in her life, thinking, how arrogant must I be to think I can handle all of this on my own?

Sitting herself on a wooden bench that looked upon the shore, Fuchsia sighed. Her thoughts were loud and scattered, as always -- missing her sisters, missing the bottom of the ocean, missing her whole mermaid world -- but most of all, missing the Captain. She also thought of Zale and wondered why he stood out from all the other humans.

Once again, Fuchsia pathetically whimpered, "Captain, where are you!?"

Just then, a beautiful girl approached Fuchsia. She was breath-taking. Her hair was a rainbow -- red at the roots, orange and yellow in the middle, green towards the bottom, and blue and purple at the tips that hung down to her belly button.

"Hi, darling," she greeted in the friendliest voice.

"Hey!" Fuchsia beamed.

"You look quite lonely," she observed.

Fuchsia was astounded. It was the first human to ever approach her, without her approaching first. She felt a strong energy from her, oddly similar to how she felt around Zale. It was as if they had already known each other from before.

"I am," Fuchsia revealed.

"My name is Rainbow."

"Just like your hair!" Fuchsia imagined that Rainbow could also be a mermaid in disguise, there was something so magical about her. "I'm Fuchsia."

"Nice to meet you. First time visiting? I get the feeling that you're new here."

"Yes!" Fuchsia widened her eyes, "I am! This is only my third day here." She wondered how she knew, and why she was being so kind and welcoming.

"I'm about to go swimming, would you like to join?" Rainbow offered.

"I don't know how to swim," Fuchsia admitted, which felt incredibly strange to say. But now that her tail was gone, she couldn't trust herself in the water anymore.

"It's perfectly fine," Rainbow convinced, her hazel eyes sparkling, "I was just going to dip my toes in."

"Alright!" Fuchsia agreed.

So the two girls headed over to the beach. They were stopped by a lifeguard at the entrance, and Rainbow flashed her bracelet, adding, "she's my guest."

With a nod, the lifeguard let them step off the boardwalk and onto the hot sand.

"What was that?" Fuchsia questioned.

"You have to pay to get on the beach during daylight hours. This bracelet is my pass and I'm allowed one guest."

Astounded, Fuchsia bursted out, "pay for the beach?"

Rainbow simply nodded.

"Pay for the land you're sharing with everyone else? What *don't* you have to pay for?"

"The air..." Rainbow paused, adding, "for now," with a chuckle.

As they headed towards the water, Fuchsia was deep in her head, attempting to comprehend how humans put a price on everything. She flashed back to the hermit crab, fantasizing of setting it free.

"Brrr!" Fuchsia shouted the moment her toes hit the sea. Goose-bumps ran all the way up her spine.

The two giggled, mesmerized by the hypnotic waves rushing back and forth, the water feeling warmer each time it brushed against their feet.

What an unusual illusion, Fuchsia thought to herself. Although the water's temperature remained the same, it seemed to be warming up, when really it was her body that was adjusting to it. Inching closer, her feet completely soaked and comfortable, now her legs were feeling icy, as the water splashed her kneecaps.

"Oh, you're going in!" Rainbow called out, "don't get your dress wet. Are you wearing a bathing suit underneath?"

"Yeah!" Fuchsia nodded, sliding her dress over her shoulders and throwing it across the water, watching it land on the sand.

Rainbow widened her eyes and gasped, "that's not a bathing suit, that's your underwear!"

"What's the difference?" She asked, wearing nothing but a white bra and white underpants. Looking around, it seemed to her that everyone was wearing just about the same.

"Not much, I suppose," she shrugged with a chuckle. Rainbow was wearing a golden one-piece with small, black swim trunks.

For several minutes, the girls stood in the ocean, continuing to gradually inch further in until the water was up to their chests. Now the crashing waves were behind them, with little waves gently hitting them, lifting them up ever so slightly before re-leasing them back down to the ground with grace.

"The waves are fairly quiet today," Rainbow observed.

"What do we do if a big one comes?" Fuchsia fretted.

"We dunk!"

"But I can't breathe underwater!"

"Close your mouth and pinch your nose," Rainbow instructed, "like this," she plopped herself down, head disappearing into the abyss.

Heart racing, Fuchsia went ahead and gave it a try.

"Eeek!" She shrieked, coming back up for air. The rush of coldness was a shock to her system.

Both girls giggled, running their hands through their wet hair.

"Refreshing!" Fuchsia let out a gasp.

Her body, immersed in the sea, felt soothed and nearly numb, while her head and shoulders felt kissed by the sun.

Fuchsia couldn't help but stare at Rainbow -- she was so magnificent, with perhaps the most beautiful face a woman could ever have. Her features were the most perfect balance between soft and sharp. Her eyes carried so much depth, gracefully placed beneath bold and kempt brows. Her tan skin shimmered and sparkled in the sun. Her voluptuous body was smooth and curvy. She was flawless.

It wasn't solely her looks, but her energy that completely brought her beauty to life. It was an unexplainable, yet unmistakable, connection. These feelings went completely beyond the surface. Fuchsia knew she was in love!

"Rainbow, are you in love with anybody?" She asked, as they were treading in the water.

"No," Rainbow firmly stated.

"Have you ever been in love?" Fuchsia tilted her head.

"No," she maintained.

Astounded, she responded, "don't you ever get lonely?"

"Never."

Disappointed, Fuchsia knew there was something hiding behind Rainbow's thick exterior. It was impossible for this newfound attraction to be unrequited.

"Rainbow," Fuchsia persisted, "this is going to sound crazy," she fidgeted her fingers nervously, "I know we just met, but it feels like I've known you my whole life. It's your energy..." She paused.

"You're a lovely friend," Rainbow agreed, in such a soft and soothing voice, kindly placing her hand upon her shoulder.

"I'm just going to say it!" Fuchsia finally blurted out, "I think I'm in love with you!"

She propelled forward towards Rainbow, leaning closer, like she was hoping to kiss her.

But Rainbow stepped back.

"I'm sorry," Rainbow explained with her arms up, "I don't feel the same."

Fuchsia's heart dropped, stunned. She wasn't accustomed to rejection; it had always been the other way around.

"Oh, gosh!" She threw her hands over her face, attempting to quickly recover, "I'm so embarrassed, please forgive me!"

"No, sweetie," she shook her head calmly, "there's no need to be upset."

Fuchsia took a heavy sigh, sadness falling over her completely.

"Let's take a break from swimming," Rainbow offered.

"Yeah, sure," Fuchsia agreed.

XI. THE FRIED FOOD TRIAD

uchsia and Rainbow gradually made their way out of the water and back to the dry sand. On her way, Fuchsia grabbed her white dress and threw it back on real fast. The two girls continued walking back to the busy boardwalk.

"Care for lunch?" Rainbow proposed.

"I'd love to!" Fuchsia rubbed her empty belly, before quickly remembering that she didn't have any money to pay for lunch. "Wait," she halted, "I don't have any money. I mean, right before you introduced yourself to me, I was actually looking for a job."

"I'll pay for both of us," Rainbow promised, "it's my treat."

"I can't," Fuchsia adamantly declined, "I can't keep relying on the kindness of strangers to take care of me. It's making me feel so pathetic."

"Honey, you don't have a pathetic bone in your body."

"I really need to get myself a job. Surely, there must be hundreds of these shops," Fuchsia pointed out as they continued strolling down the boardwalk, "one of them is bound to accept me. And if all else fails, maybe I'll become a lifeguard with Zale. But I really need to do this myself."

"You can't job search on an empty stomach. Have lunch with me, and then I'll set you free, and hopefully we'll meet again."

Fuchsia sighed -- somehow, she could not resist Rainbow's charm -- so she caved, "okay, let's eat," with a half-smile.

And so, the two ladies settled for a low-key seafood restaurant, sitting at a patio table with an umbrella overhead to shield them from the scorching sun.

Scanning the menu, Fuchsia's eyes widened, "the '*fried food triad*'? Fried ravioli, mozzarella sticks, and fish sticks!?" She began to drool.

"Sounds good!" Rainbow cheered, "let's go for it!"

"Are you sure?"

"Yes! But I'm also going to order us a salad so you get your vegetables," she added.

"Blah," Fuchsia stuck out her tongue and rolled her eyes.

After the waiter took their orders, Fuchsia took a sip of her ice water before clearing her throat, shifting into a serious tone, "Rainbow," she began, "can I ask why you didn't want to kiss me? Are you really not interested? Is it because I'm a girl?"

"It's not that," Rainbow shook her head, "truthfully, it doesn't matter to me what gender you are. I'm simply not interested, and that's all. Don't take it personally."

Leaning in closer with frustration, Fuchsia replied, "okay, but how can I not take it personally when you're literally rejecting my personality? Unless it's my looks -- but that can't be possible," she let out a forced laughter.

"Fuchsia, you're a very cute girl. But you're not my type."

"Not your type!?" Fuchsia's jaw dropped, "I'm *everyone's* type! Everybody loves me!"

Rainbow giggled, "you're quite full of yourself, huh?"

"Nuh-uh," Fuchsia crossed her arms, "it's only the truth!"

"Have you never been rejected before?"

"Never!"

"And what about the Captain?" She raised an eyebrow.

"The... the Captain?" Fuchsia stuttered in shock, "how did you... how did you know?"

Rainbow casually shrugged.

Just then, the waiter arrived with their giant platter of fried goodness, along with a large bowl full of vegetables.

Widening her eyes again, Fuchsia gushed, "mmm," taking in the delicious, oily smell. Reaching her hand in without restraint, she screamed, "*OUCH*! It's hot!"

"Careful now," Rainbow gestured, "let it cool down. Be patient."

"I am *so hungry!*" Fuchsia whined like a child.

"Have some salad first," Rainbow offered.

"Fine," Fuchsia scooped up some lettuce and threw it on her plate.

Rainbow slowly shook her head with a giggle.

"Wait," Fuchsia backtracked, after getting distracted by the food, "how do you know about the Captain? Are you one of his girl-friends, or something?" Fuchsia ground her teeth with envy.

"Nope."

"Then what is it? Do you know Zale, did he tell you about me?

Can you read minds or something?" Fuchsia suddenly became extremely paranoid. She knew it -- she knew that Rainbow was hiding some type of secret. There was something about her that seemed so closed off.

"I think the food's ready to eat now," Rainbow reached in for a ravioli and dipped it in the marinara sauce.

"Don't change the subject," Fuchsia furrowed her eyebrows.

"Okay, here's the truth," Rainbow let out a short sigh, "I'm magic."

"You're a mermaid?"

"Something like that."

"I knew it!" Fuchsia bursted out loud, smacking her hands on the table, "tell me *everything*!"

"Let's change the subject -- I wanna get to know you, girl to girl. Tell me more about yourself."

"No!" Fuchsia exclaimed, "I'm getting to the bottom of this!"

"Fuch, I wanna know you better. Make me change my mind about you. Maybe you're my type, afterall," she winked.

"Stop!" Fuchsia persisted, "I don't like being kept in the dark like this. What do you know about the Captain?"

"Oh, forget him!" She rolled her eyes, growing frustrated, "I want to know *you*. Tell me, why do you hide behind your looks?"

"Hide behind my looks? Excuse me?"

"Yeah, you seem to use your beauty as a distraction from your personality."

Taken aback, Fuchsia defended herself, "well, that's a very rude thing to say -- coming from the girl with no personality," she gave a dirty look.

"I'm sorry, I didn't mean to insult you," Rainbow sincerely apologized.

"I don't think I'm the most beautiful girl to exist -- I mean look at you, you're *way* prettier than me! Honestly, I don't know what it is. I put a spell on everyone, it's like I'm cursed! If you were a man, surely you'd be drooling over me."

"You think every man is in love with you, huh?"

"Of course not!" Fuchsia furrowed her eyebrows, "I think most are infatuated with me. There's a difference. It's all just lust, and that's not what I'm looking for."

"What are you looking for, then?"

"I want true love -- in the cheesiest, cringiest, most unrealistic way possible. I want to be rescued like a princess. I have all the fairytales memorized by heart -- I used to be an actress back home, reenacting them in one-woman shows."

"You do all these shows yourself? No supporting actors?"

"That's right."

"Why's that? You don't like to share the spotlight?"

"No, you're wrong -- it's not that. It's because..." Fuchsia stared into the distance with wonder, "...nobody shares the same vision as me. No one takes it seriously enough, no one understands the message. I wasn't just doing these shows for fun, I was trying to teach my merpeople something -- that love is real and worth fighting for -- that there's more to life than eating all day and partying all night."

Sensing the urgency in her tone, Rainbow responded with, "wow, you're very passionate about your plays."

"I *was*..." Fuchsia bowed her head, "and then the Captain broke my heart... And I thought, what's the point? It's all just enter-tainment to them. I don't wanna merely make them laugh... I want to make a difference."

"That's beautiful."

"Thanks," Fuchsia said, chowing down on her meal.

The two were quiet for a moment while they ate, before Rainbow continued, "tell me what's going with the Captain," she lifted her shoulders in excitement, "sounds like a scandalous love affair," she teased.

"Girl, I wish," Fuchsia lifted up her hands with an attitude.

"What's going on? Tell me all the deets!"

"I don't know what you've heard, or who told you what, but he did *not* reject me like you insinuated."

"Hmm?" Rainbow tilted her head.

"He's just..." Fuchsia paused to gather her thoughts, "he's... un-sure, I think... I mean, he told me..." it was so difficult for her to get her words out, but she pushed through, "he told me he was in love with me," and as soon as she said it out loud, her heart sank -- it was unreal. Fuchsia felt her face turn as red as a tomato.

Rainbow pleasantly nodded, continuing to give Fuchsia room to speak more.

"I mean, I've been told 'I love you' before, but never like this... not only was it love at first sight, it just hit me harder. At first, I didn't believe him. But the more I thought about it, the more I realized he had nothing to gain, except me."

"So... what's the problem?"

"I had my chance -- to join his ship and sail away together -- but I didn't trust him. And then he had his chance -- to meet me at the Mermaid Ball -- but he didn't trust me. So then, Mother Mermaid heard my cries, and she gave me a chance -- to prove myself. And that's why I'm here with the humans. Not only had I grown bored and tired of the mermaid world, I also wanted to show the Captain that I can work through my fears and he doesn't have to worry about scaring me away."

"Aha," Rainbow nodded, their plate now nearly empty. "You know what I think?"

"What!?"

"I think you have more than proven yourself."

"But this whole time, I've been surviving on the kindness of strangers and lucky breaks. I need to really show him that I can do this myself -- I'll find my own job, my own place to live, I'll do it all on my own."

"You say you wanna be rescued -- you can't be rescued if you insist on doing everything all by yourself," Rainbow pointed out.

Fuchsia paused for a moment before admitting, "I suppose there's some truth to that."

"So," Rainbow gathered, "you left your safe world behind, your world of fun and play, in order to survive out here in 'the human world,' or 'the real world,' or 'the wilderness' -- whatever you call it -- without anyone else's help."

"Exactly," Fuchsia nodded, before adding, "well, technically Mother Mermaid forced me to do so. This is never something I would've chosen myself! But she knew that it was precisely what I needed in order to fulfill my destiny. I trust the goddess of the sea and her plans for me. And I seriously believe that the Captain is the key to my destiny."

"And you think this is what will bring you two together?"

"Yes," she passionately nodded, "I was so scared when I first met him, but now I'm becoming so much stronger, I know I can be brave enough for him, now!"

Rainbow pulled out her wallet and threw some cash on the table, tucking it under the empty plate, "I say, forget that job search. You've already proven yourself. My intuition is strong and I truly feel that the Captain is waiting for you, and he cannot wait any longer! He's ready!"

"You really think so?" Fuchsia was never one to trust strangers, but Rainbow was no stranger -- she was a long-lost soulmate -- and she was magic, afterall.

"Yes!" Rainbow grinned, "I *know* so!"

"But I've been waiting for him to show up here, and he hasn't!"

"Then go find him yourself! Go find your Captain before it's too late!"

"Okay!" Fuchsia stood tall, jumping out of her seat.

"Come with me," Rainbow whispered, grabbed her hand, and led her away from the restaurant and out into a grassy field.

"Where are we going!?" Fuchsia laughed, as the two of them began running, giggling hand in hand.

"You'll see!" Rainbow cheered.

Out of nowhere, Fuchsia lost all sight of her surroundings. She heard the sound of a wave creeping up behind her. Turning around, wide-eyed, she felt a rush of water pour over her with rage. The next thing she knew, there was total darkness. Rainbow was gone. There Fuchsia stood, all alone.

XII. RETURN OF
THE CAPTAIN

Nothing but darkness surrounded Fuchsia... until a small light appeared in the distance, growing larger and brighter before her eyes.

And then appeared Mother Mermaid herself, in all her beauty and wonder!

"Welcome home, Fuchsia. You did it! You immersed yourself into a brand new adventure with confidence and bravery! You have proven to me that you truly have what it takes. I have great plans for you, my mermaid, and I know you will not let me down."

Fuchsia was speechless. She looked down and noticed that her tail was back. She pulled a chunk of hair and saw it was vividly pink again. And her skin, glowing. Her mermaid magic had fully returned!

"You do not have to tell me what it means to be a mermaid," Mother Mermaid declared, "you showed that to me through your actions: your kindness, your loyalty, and your unshakable intuition."

All Fuchsia could do was nod. She was absolutely speechless and still in shock over what was happening.

"And you never gave up," Mother Mermaid concluded.

It was incomprehensible for Fuchsia to believe that it had only been a few days that she had lived as a human among other humans on land. For, it had seemed so much longer than that. She wasn't even sure when, or if, she would ever return home. Instead, her mind had been overly preoccupied with either the Captain, or her new and strange surroundings. There hadn't been any time for her to ponder if Mother Mermaid would ever bring her back home. Still processing everything, she took a sigh of relief.

"Now," Mother Mermaid continued, "your journey has only just begun."

"Mother Mermaid," Fuchsia pleaded, "I want to see the Captain. I love him. Can you please bring him to me?" She clasped her hands together in prayer.

"One step at a time!" She commanded.

"What's next?" Fuchsia cried in dismay, "what are these 'plans' you have for me? And, also... *why me?*"

"Why 'you'? I have already explained to you that you are remarkably different from the rest, that you are the only one who can handle this goddess-given destiny. My plans for you are grand. And what's next, is that you shall be queen of the sea!"

"Queen!?" Fuchsia felt her heart sink, attempting to catch her breath.

"There is no one more deserving than you, Fuchsia. Your heart is pure and persevering like no one else's. You shall rule the sea, guide the merpeople, and be their great leader."

"I-I don't know if I can do that," she stuttered nervously.

"You can survive the human world -- you can do *anything*."

"Mother Mermaid, I really don't think I can..."

Cutting her off, she barked, "this is not a request; this is a *demand!*"

Fuchsia pressed her lips together anxiously.

Mother Mermaid explained, "your first task as queen is to give your merpeople a speech."

"A speech!?"

"Yes, a speech. I want you to speak your truth, tell the mermaids and mermen your story, and share with them my message."

"Uh," Fuchsia hesitated, "and what message is that, exactly?"

"Speak from your heart, and my message will naturally come through."

Gulping at her lack of specificity, Fuchsia hoped, "maybe you can just tell them yourself."

Mother Mermaid roared back, "I am *always* sharing my message with the world. But most are not willing to listen, unable to open their third eyes and see the truth. You have proven yourself to be the only one fit to be my messenger. With your help, you can act as the medium for my words."

"I understand," Fuchsia replied, "I'm just not exactly sure what I'm supposed to tell them."

"As I said -- tell them your story, speak from your heart, and the truth will come through on its own. I trust in you, Fuchsia."

"Where is the Captain? Will he be there in the crowd? I'd really rather not give a speech, I just want to talk to him, just the two of us!" Fuchsia whined.

"You can't -- not just yet!"

"Why not!?"

"You will ruin my plans -- your destiny!"

Fuchsia impatiently moaned, "but I want to be with him *now!*"

"Listen, child!" Mother Mermaid furiously explained, "I am Goddess! That means, I am all-wise, all-knowing, and all-seeing! I see what's in your heart, and I know you better than you do. Therefore, I create your destiny. If you ruin any step of the plan, you ruin your destiny!"

Fuchsia thought back on what Madame, the old psychic, had told her. It was essentially the opposite -- that Fuchsia was not special, and that destiny was a choice one made.

Fuchsia bowed her head, showing a bit more humility now, before replying in a softer tone, "with all due respect, it's arguable that destiny is changeable -- that whatever is given to me, I can choose whether I consent to it or not."

"You must understand that your conscious mind is limited -- as goddess, it is my responsibility to intervene with the affairs of the mermaids and mermen. The ocean would be far more chaotic without my assistance. Not so long ago, you were praying for my help. And that's what I'm doing, child, I'm helping. The more you try to control my plans, the more you defeat yourself. Destiny is unstoppable because I make it so. Yet those who stir things, rock the boat."

"I see," she sighed.

"Put your faith in me. I know you want to be with the Captain right now, but you're going to have to be patient. It's all very confusing right now, but with time, you'll understand."

"I sure hope so," she sighed.

"Promise me that you and the Captain will stay away from each other until I make it clear that you are both ready," Mother Mermaid ordered, "I don't want either of you wrecking my plans for you both."

"Do I really have to?" Fuchsia groaned.

"Yes, promise!"

"But, I love the Captain! If you really want us to be together, then why are you keeping us apart?"

"I don't have to explain everything to you," Mother Mermaid scowled, "and even if I did, you wouldn't understand. I've already explained myself enough. You two are simply not ready right now, and that's all there is to it. I know you're both anxious."

"He's anxious too!?" Fuchsia perked up, "what else about the Captain? Does he miss me? How much does he think about me?"

"That's enough!" Mother Mermaid nearly screamed, "it's time for you to give your first speech as queen!"

"Wait!" Fuchsia stalled, "can I at least see my sisters first? Please? I miss them so much."

"Your sisters have swam across the ocean. I promise you'll see them again soon."

"Swam across the ocean!? Well, why in the world would they do that!?" She tilted her head in complete bewilderment.

"Focus!" Mother Mermaid barked back, "I need you to focus right now on your entire mermaid and mermen family as a collective whole."

"Alright, I'll do it, I'll be queen," she reluctantly agreed -- as if she even had a choice.

And the next thing she knew, she was standing on the largest rock, looking down upon millions of mermaids and mermen.

Fuchsia began trembling with anxiety. She was used to crowds, but none ever this big. The crowd was absolutely silent, hypnotically staring at her, wide-eyed, as if a spell had been casted upon them.

She thought to herself -- *everyone thinks I'm so arrogant and self-centered. They say -- 'oh, you only want one boyfriend, one husband, one true love... oh, you only do one-woman shows.' Just because I'm an actress, just because I'm charming and have a way with others -- it doesn't mean I'm a narcissist.*

They'd think I would die to be queen, but I'm not fit to rule. I've always been my own queen, always hoped to be one man's queen someday, yet never strived to be everyone else's. And now, here I am, queen of all the sea.

Snapping herself out of her daze, it was time to finally speak.

With a deep breath, Fuchsia began, "mermaids and mermen, I'm here to tell you my story," Her voice was shaky. The silence remained.

She cleared her throat and continued, "I met Mother Mermaid in the flesh, face to face. For anyone who doubts her existence, I can assure you that she is real," Fuchsia shot her arms up with passion, unaware of the flames that would burst through her palms.

Gasps!

Raising her eyebrows, in awe of herself, Fuchsia carried on, "and she cast me away from this seafoam society to live among the humans as one of them for a couple of days."

She started hearing quiet chatter form in the back.

"I was sick of living as a mermaid, sick of swimming in circles all day... and Mother Mermaid had heard my cries! She sent me on a mission to see if I could survive being a human, and I did! I have gone to the other side and back. And I made it. Here I am, still alive!"

Fuchsia impulsively stomped her fin on the rock she floated upon, provoking a bolt of lightning to strike.

More gasps!

Fuchsia had no idea what was happening to her, all she knew was that she couldn't stop, "I have learned that humans are distracted, stupid, and lonely! They put a price on everything -- on food, on all their items, on free roaming animals, even on the land itself, on the sand and the sea. It's harsh out there, and even the humans themselves are afraid of their own breed."

More chatter rising.

"But it's not as terrible as it seems. I met some kind souls. And what I've learned is that, you must work through your fears in life, you must be brave. We don't have to hide in fear anymore. If we could all come together in bravery, we could rise to the human world and teach them our ways! We can show them that materialism and money doesn't matter! We can set them free!"

In return, the crowd broke into a riot. Half of them welcomed her message, applauding and cheering with tears of joy — while the other half became even more fearful, booing and yelling. The next thing she knew, violence broke out. Mermaids and mermen were taking swings at one another, even the innocent children were getting pushed around.

Fuchsia felt her face go pale, watching her worst fear come true: letting Mother Mermaid down. Surely, this is not what the legendary goddess had envisioned, right?

"Stop!" Fuchsia panicked, attempting to control them. But of course, no one could hear her.

"STOP!!!" she tried again, this time at the top of her lungs. And still, the riot continued. It was a full-on mosh pit.

She threw her arms up again, provoking another burst of flames, but this only caused the crowd to become more aggressive. It occurred to her that she needed to calm them down somehow.

Fuchsia began to sing. As her voice grew louder, the crowd became a bit quieter. So she continued singing, as loudly as she could, like that day when she was all alone on the rock before she had first met the Captain. Her voice echoed through the sea, and the merpeople were now turning their attention back to her.

Fuchsia did a little twirl, and now they were nearly silent. She continued singing, dancing around, and sure enough they were completely mesmerized. It was an absolutely incredible feeling, the power of having so many souls under her control.

"Queen!" Someone shouted, "make her our queen!"

More joined in, chanting, "queen! Queen! Queen!"

Fuchsia was flabbergasted, but she wouldn't let herself fight against it -- she soaked it all in.

A group of merpeople rushed to her side to place a jeweled crown on her head. The silver tiara rested nicely on top of her pink hair. Looking around, there were so many eyes staring at her. And she had control over all of them. Adrenaline rushed through her veins. Fuchsia felt as if she had died and gone to heaven, it was all too perfect.

Breaking out of her trance, Fuchsia was distracted by a flash of light in the corner of her eye. She looked upwards towards the light, noticing it was shining from above the shore. Like a moth to a flame, she felt uncontrollably drawn to it, and began to swim away from her merpeople in order to chase this light.

"I'll be back," she called out to them.

"We'll be here!" A few cried out, "working on your gifts!"

Fuchsia's mind went completely blank as she continued swimming away from the bottom of the ocean, and steadily towards the surface. She was like a cat chasing a laser toy.

Coming up for air, she froze -- there he was... the Captain...

He was standing there on his ship, looking down with a smile -- a very serious smile. He reached out his hand, and Fuchsia grabbed it without question, plopping herself on the boat.

"My mermaid," he passionately greeted her.

"My Captain," she responded without a second thought.

"Come away with me," he demanded with a dreamy tone in his voice.

Fuchsia started to nod until she stopped herself -- snapping out of a haze -- blinking several times before saying, "wait!"

"What is it?" He furrowed his eyebrows.

"What's going on?" She panicked, "wh-why now?" She stuttered in fear and confusion, "I-I kept waiting for you, on that little rock, and you just kept sailing by!"

"I'm here now," he firmly stated.

"And then I was ready to jump on your ship, but you were with someone else!"

"I'm here now," he simply repeated.

"I left the ocean, I joined the humans, and..."

Attempting to silence her, the Captain rushed on for a fiery kiss.

But Fuchsia stopped him, "no!" She screamed, pushing his face away.

He stepped back, his expression turned heavy.

"They just made me their queen, and now you're here to take me away? I've finally found joy, and you're here to ruin it? I watched you sail past me every day, that's when you were supposed to come and rescue me. I was cast to live with the humans these past few days, where were you *then*, huh?"

"Darling, I know more than you think," he expressed confidently.

"What are you talking about? You're not human, are you?" She freaked out.

"I was once a merman."

"What!?"

"Will you let me explain?"

"Sure," she sighed.

The Captain stood tall, beginning his tale, "a long, long time ago — long before your time, I was a merman. It was hundreds of years ago."

"Hundreds of years ago!?" Fuchsia cut him off in astonishment, "you-you're *how old*, now?"

"Does it matter?" he asked.

"I know merpeople can live up to a thousand years -- or even longer than that, before our water became so polluted."

"I'm certainly far, far younger than a thousand years old..."

"You look like... I dunno... thirties?"

"So I've been told, I have fantastic genes."

"I'm turning twenty, soon."

"Shall I continue my tale, now?"

"Yes," Fuchsia nodded, before adding, "what *else* haven't you mentioned?"

"Oh, you just wait. As I was saying..."

Fuchsia nodded.

The Captain followed, "upon my entrance into adulthood, Mother Mermaid called on me. She determined that I had what it took to be the messenger of the goddess, to share her message with the world -- peace and bravery. And just as these ones have made you queen, they did the same to me, making me king.

"But very quickly, they lost sight. They worshipped *me*, instead of *my message*. And it messed with my head. They fed my ego until I exploded. I thought I was invincible. The message was therefore lost.

"The only way out was: faking my death and fleeing. I disguised my identity as a captain and went on to spend my days sailing the world. But I'm not out looking for gold or treasures, like other captains, I'm out here looking for love. And I've found that you're the greatest treasure of all."

Fuchsia couldn't help but feel warm and fuzzy, butterflies dancing in her stomach. How charming he was, she thought, and how impressive was his story. She looked deep in his eyes, yearning to embrace him.

"So, join me," he concluded.

Fuchsia turned her head around to look at the clear, blue sea. Back home, awaited her sisters, her merpeople friends, and a new life full of riches. It was comfortable, it was everything she had been trying to get away from, but now it was offering her more than ever. It was her chance to be a hero, messenger of the great Mother Mermaid, countless divine rewards awaiting her. If the Captain was right, then it would be nothing but disaster. But if he was telling her a fib, then this was indeed her chance to save the world -- let the merpeople and the humans coexist together in peace, let her lead the legacy of victory.

And then Fuchsia turned her head back to look at her Captain and his ship. Here, there was adventure -- but full of so many unknowns. There was hardly any trust. For all she knew, he could end up hurting her, tying her up, and exploiting her for her magic. His story could have easily been a lie, and he was actually a normal human, desperate to take advantage of her.

He silently stood there with patience, letting Fuchsia think. But time was ticking, and she needed to make a decision fast. Her merpeople were waiting for her, yet the Captain was waiting for her too. It all came down to this: loyalty to her species, or loyalty to this strange man who she felt an illogically strong connection with?

With a heavy sigh, Fuchsia professed, "Mother Mermaid told me that we must take this time apart before we reconnect. She said we're not ready yet. I don't understand her, and I'm dying to jump into your arms, but my heart is telling me that I have to trust her plan."

"Don't listen to the goddess," the Captain urged, "she's not as wise as she believes. She thinks she knows best, but she doesn't. I know what's best for you, for me, for us! There's nothing stopping us now!"

"We don't know that," Fuchsia moaned, "it could quickly spiral into a disaster."

"You're making no sense!" The Captain shook his head, "don't be so scared!"

"Come with me, then!" Fuchsia suggested, "swim back with me into the sea, be a merman again, and we can rule together as king and queen!" She smiled wholeheartedly.

"No," he denied, "they'll drive us mad, they'll worship us to death, and we'll never have peace."

"But what if this is what Mother Mermaid wants for us?"

"Don't listen to Mother Mermaid! She's lying to you about me. She doesn't want us to be together -- not now, not ever! By keeping us apart, she's stalling for time until she finds a better king for you."

"What better king for me than you? I've made it clear to her how much I lo--" Fuchsia stopped herself, "how much I... want to be with you."

"How much you..." the Captain sweetly grinned, "love me?"

Fuchsia stammered, wondering how it could possibly be so difficult to say such a simple phrase to the man of her dreams, "I-I..."

"You can't even say it," the Captain sharply turned his head to the left in despair.

"Can *you*!?" Fuchsia raised her eyebrows.

"I'm not your king," he stated.

"Why not!?"

"Because I didn't pass her test!" He screamed, echoing across the ocean, "like I said, I faked my death and ran away! She's doing these things to test you, and you're going to keep on passing, and find the perfect merman who also passes all the tests!"

"Don't be so scared now, Captain."

"I'm not scared, *you're* scared," he insisted.

"I have to get back to the ocean now, back to my merpeople," Fuchsia told him, a part of her hoping that he'd stop her.

"Then, go," he motioned her away with a careless shrug.

"Seriously?" Fuchsia couldn't believe he was simply letting her go.

"If that's what you want to do, then do it. Find your king."

"*You* are my king."

"Then stay."

"I can't."

"Then *GO!*" He shouted.

And with that, Fuchsia disappeared deep into the sea and returned to her worshippers.

XIII. QUEEN FOR (HALF) A DAY

Upon returning, Fuchsia witnessed a colossal, 10,000 foot statue of herself! Every detail — from the shape of her features to every single freckle on her body — was included. Her jaw dropped in absolute disbelief.

"Queen," a merman said to her, "all ten thousand of us carved this in your honor. Are you pleased?"

"Of course!" Fuchsia exclaimed in total delight.

"Queen," another merman rushed to her side, "I wrote a hundred poems about your beauty. May I recite them to you?"

"Why, most certainly!" She blushed.

"Queen!" A mermaid cut in, "I put together a brand new wardrobe of seashell bras for you to wear, tailored to your exact measurements! Would you like to model them for me?"

"I'd love to!" She cheered.

"Queen!" A very pregnant mermaid said, "I'm pregnant with quintuplets and I plan on naming *ALL* of my children 'Fuchsia' in your honor! May you bless the babies by rubbing my stomach?"

"Sure!" She rubbed the woman's stomach, "you're going to name them *all* 'Fuchsia,' how will you tell them apart?"

"Queen!" The head scientist said, "we've started a space program with plans to start a colony on Neptune — you know, the ocean planet — and make you queen there as well!"

"Oh, my goodness!" She exclaimed, "but shouldn't we focus on Earth first? The humans..."

"Queen!" Another shouted.

"Hold on, hold on!" She screamed. "What about my plans? To unite with the humans?"

"Gosh queen, we have no time for that!" They explained, "we must spend all of our time pleasing you!"

Fuchsia's head was spinning; she was so overwhelmed. Everyone was staring at her, ready to do whatever she commanded them to.

"You don't understand," Fuchsia attempted to explain, "this is not about me, this is about all of us! World peace is a group effort! I can't do this all alone!"

"So, you must have a king by your side!" They decided. "Who would you like as your king?"

Fuchsia slapped herself, trying to wake up from this madness.

"Has anyone seen my sisters?" She whimpered.

"Fuchsia!" Marino called out.

Fuchsia was never so relieved to see a recognizable face, calling back, "hey! Marino! Please people, let him by!"

Emerging from the crowd came Marino, along with friends Finn and Gill.

"Fuchsia, ever since you left the ocean, your sisters went out searching for you. We haven't seen them since!" Marino explained.

Her heart pounded.

"It's only been a couple days, though," Finn added, trying to be positive, "I'm sure they'll be back soon."

Another merman cut in, "so, Fuchsia, which one of these fellows shall be your king?"

Fuchsia stared at the three boys in bafflement.

"Make me your king," Marino begged, "I've known you longest."

"No, me!" Finn exclaimed, "I know you best."

"No, choose me!" Gill yelled, "I appreciate you the most!"

"I already have a king!" Fuchsia screamed.

"Who is it?" Marino asked, "and where is he?"

"He's..." Fuchsia awkwardly explained, "he's not here right now."

"When will he get here?"

"Never," she hopelessly sighed, "he said he doesn't want to be my king."

"Then let me be your king," Marino demanded.

"No way, dude," Finn cut in, "Fuchsia wants to be with *me*."

"She's mine," Gill whined.

"You know what!?" Fuchsia yelped, "fine! Marino! You can be my king, I guess! Everyone else -- leave me alone!"

"Give the lady some space!" Marino ordered, as he swam away with Fuchsia to find some privacy.

Instantly, Fuchsia felt herself overcome with dread. Something was severely off. Her head was spinning. She could not deny that the Captain was right -- they'd never follow through on her vision to unite with the humans, they were too wrapped up in worshipping her now.

Marino began, "Fuchsia, I am so sorry that I took you for granted. I've been thinking, and I really want to..."

"Dude, just shut up!" Fuchsia burst out.

"Huh!?" Marino was completely taken aback.

"You're not my king -- I just said that so we could get some darn peace and quiet. Marino, this was a huge mistake. I've gotta get out of here!" She panicked.

"What is going on!?"

"I wish I could tell you."

"Fuchsia, this is perfect -- you and me, king and queen of the sea. Imagine our life together, so safe and protected."

"This is not what I want," she shook her head.

"It's not?"

"No, my heart belongs to someone else..." Fuchsia bowed her head, "but I don't know if we'll ever be together."

"Then be with me, Fuchsia," Marino insisted, "I'm right here, right now."

"I'm so confused and overwhelmed, I have no idea what's going on right now!" Fuchsia cried out, "one minute I'm living among the humans, the next minute I'm getting harassed by millions of merpeople who are somehow hypnotized," she sighed, "can you please give me some space to clear my head?"

"Of course," Marino nodded, "go take some space and think it over, we'll all be here waiting for you."

Fuchsia gulped as she watched Marino swim back towards the mad crowd.

"Mother Mermaid!?" Fuchsia shouted, "I need to talk to you! Can you please come here!?"

Fuchsia waited, but there was no response. It was just her and the darkness of the sea.

And so, she continued talking to herself, "I'm sorry, I'm not fit to be queen, okay!? Everyone here is completely out of control! It's terrifying!"

Fuchsia waited... and still, no answer.

"Mother Mermaid!" Fuchsia went on, hoping she could still hear her somehow, even though she wouldn't show herself, "I know it's not in your so-called plans, but I need to get back to the Captain! I'd be a fool to let him go again!"

More silence.

"I'm dead serious!" She emphasized.

Fuchsia stood there, waiting for Mother Mermaid's fury, but there was yet no response. So, she took a breath of relief. It was time to sail away with the Captain once and for all. This time, no more distractions getting in the way.

Swimming as fast as she could, Fuchsia made her way back to where the Captain was, praying he'd still be there. Panic overflowed her, like she had once again lost a perfect opportunity.

Please still be here, please!

And to her absolute luck, there he was, standing proudly on his ship. It was as if, in that short timespan, he hadn't even moved an inch. It was like he knew that she would quickly change her mind and run right back to him.

"You're still here!" Fuchsia bursted with joy.

"That was fast," he smirked, "and yes, of course I'm still here. I can't leave your side Fuchsia, it's physically impossible."

"Is it too late?"

"It's never too late when you're in love. Love is boundless, it has no deadline."

"You love me," Fuchsia grinned.

"I love you so much," he poured out, like he had been holding it inside of him for far too long.

"I love you more," Fuchsia replied without hesitation. She glowed, collapsing into his big arms.

"Let's sail away, my mermaid," he picked her up and carried her onto his grand boat.

"Oh, my Captain," Fuchsia gushed, still in his arms, "I won't listen to Mother Mermaid. You were right -- she was trying to keep us apart, trying to entice me away with fame and fortune, but I won't do it. I don't care what she says, no matter how powerful she may be. Any 'plan' that keeps me apart from you is a plan that I refuse to follow."

Placing her down, the Captain shifted into worry when he asked, "is it true, though?"

"Is 'what' true?"

"That you really wanted to guide the merpeople into uniting with the humans? I mean, if they hadn't been so obsessed with you, and actually listened to what you had to say, would you still have come back for me?"

"Of course!" Fuchsia insisted.

"How do I know that?" He questioned.

"Because I'm here!" Fuchsia exclaimed, "does it even matter!? We have to stop doing this -- we have to stop spoiling the moment with overthinking!"

"I can't help but feel that I'm kidnapping you from your home, that I'm taking you away from your dream."

"I mean," Fuchsia sighed, "in a perfect world, the sea people and land people could coexist as one. But it's just not realistic. I was only doing what I thought Mother Mermaid wanted, and now I realize that I can't trust her. I want to be with you, and that's all. Everyone else can fend for themselves."

The Captain looked down in disappointment, "so you're settling for me..."

"I am *not* settling!" Fuchsia insisted, slapping her hands together in frustration, "I want to be with you! That's all I've ever wanted since we first met!"

"You still don't trust me, though."

"Yes I do!"

"No," he argued, "I warned you that being queen was a horrible mistake, and you went ahead and tried it anyway."

"But I realized right away that you were right! I *do* trust you, Captain, I *really do*!"

The Captain sighed.

Fuchsia continued, "you're spoiling the moment! This is here and now! Don't you dare push me away again!" She exclaimed, "let's rebel against our great goddess!"

"Alright!" The Captain suddenly snapped out of his paranoid haze, "let's do it!" He raised his fist in exaltation.

"This is it," Fuchsia braced herself, "this is our time!"

Fuchsia could infer that there was still some hesitation and insecurity getting in the way, yet determined that they would push through it. Like running into a fire, love was calling for them, and they couldn't resist.

It didn't matter if Mother Mermaid insisted that they weren't ready yet, that they still had more tests to pass before they could live happily ever after. She thought -- how hard could true love be, anyway? She didn't need anyone else's blessings or approval, even from the great goddess Herself.

"Anchor's away!" The Captain announced, beginning to set sail.

XIV. OCEANA PARADISE

Fuchsia rested herself on the bow of the ship -- a perfect view of the sea. The sun was setting and the sky was cotton candy pink.

She turned around to see her handsome Captain behind her, steering the wheel with confidence. It was glorious to see him taking control, making her feel safe and protected. She didn't know where they were going, but now she trusted him. After realizing how wise he was, and how deeply he cared for her, she wasn't worried anymore. It was like a switch had flipped.

Staring into the distance, Fuchsia imagined kissing her Captain. The thought of it made her a nervous wreck, her palms getting clammy and her heartbeat pulsing through her arms and legs, chills running down her spine.

She had kissed several boys in her past, but now it had been quite some time since. Plus there was something obviously different about the Captain; he wasn't like any other boy she had known. And while they had already shared one kiss together over a year ago, things were different now -- she was far more invested and there was much more at stake.

Shifting uncomfortably in her seat, anxiety was dominantly creeping over her. Fuchsia placed her hand on her stomach as it rumbled. With each breath, her lungs constricted a little tighter.

Attempting to relax, she took in a long inhale and then exhaled deeply.

Thoughts of kissing the Captain persisted -- but it wasn't a dreamy fantasy anymore, it was now reality.

What if he doesn't like the way I kiss? What if I'm a bad kisser? What if I don't do it right?

As much as she attempted to quiet down the fretful noise inside her head, her worries only grew stronger.

Fuchsia forced herself to turn around and look at the Captain again, hoping his warm face would calm her down. But instead, he didn't look quite so confident anymore, as she observed his shaky hands struggling to grasp the wheel. He was losing control of the ship. There was sweat dripping down from his forehead, his face beaming red.

"A-are you okay?" Fuchsia stuttered.

"I'm fine," he sharply insisted.

"You look nervous," she quietly murmured under her breath.

"What?" He asked, unable to hear her.

"Nothing," Fuchsia forced an awkward smile.

Stop overthinking, she told herself, *don't ruin this!*

The boat started rocking back and forth, so much now that Fuchsia feared they were going to tip over!

"What's wrong with your ship?" Fuchsia asked, as panic began to prevail.

"It's just some rough waters," he flatly explained, focusing hard on the ocean ahead of him, avoiding eye contact with his mermaid. "I assure you, I'm a great sailor."

"Well, can you stop it from rocking so much?" Fuchsia panted, "I'm really seasick."

"I'm trying!" He barked back.

Now Fuchsia's nausea was growing even stronger. The taste of acid traveled up her throat, causing her to clench over and cover her mouth in order to stop herself from vomiting.

"I think I'm gonna throw up," she groaned.

"This has never happened before," the Captain mumbled to himself -- this was not the way he ever imagined sailing his mermaid away. It was supposed to be a smooth ride into the sunset, birds flying above them, and then he would anchor them down on a private beach where they could finally share that perfect kiss... but now, the boat was rocking side to side and his steering wheel was spinning out of control.

He grasped his wheel even harder now, clenching with all his might, yet his hands continued shaking uncontrollably. The Captain felt Fuchsia's eyes on him -- watching him panic, watching him lose control. The more she stared, the more the sweat poured down his face, the more his body trembled in fear.

As much as he told himself to stay calm, he couldn't. Fuchsia had been right, he determined, his overthinking was his greatest enemy. He wanted to smash his mind and slash his thoughts so that his heart could peacefully enjoy this moment. And still, he continued losing control. His mermaid's mesmerizing beauty took power over him. Her wide eyes laying upon him felt like a blinding spotlight shining on him -- he couldn't bear it, he had to squint his eyes and look away.

And now, looking up, clouds rolled in rapidly and the pink sky transformed to dark blue. It looked like a storm was headed their way at full speed.

Gusts of wind rushed in, causing the boat to tip even more, as Fuchsia shrieked while holding her stomach tight.

The Captain placed his hand on his forehead in bewilderment. All control was gone.

Suddenly, the ship came to an abrupt halt.

"What's going on?" Fuchsia panicked.

"Leave," the Captain demanded in a cold, flat voice.

"You're joking," she nervously chuckled.

"It's not a joke," he maintained.

"Huh!?" Fuchsia was completely taken aback.

"You can go now," he quietly stated.

"Are you serious!?"

"I'm dead serious."

"I don't understand," she furrowed her eyebrows, "did I do something? What's wrong?"

"JUST GO!" He screamed at the top of his lungs, emotions now pouring out of him. "Get off of my ship!" He pointed to the ocean.

Fuchsia couldn't even believe it. This couldn't be happening, this couldn't...

"Captain, we already settled this!" Fuchsia cried out, "we're sailing away together now, there's nothing stopping us!"

"I told you that you have to leave," he ordered with frustration.

"Can you at least tell me why? Can't you see how I'm so in love with you!?"

"I don't think you're ready for this," he avoided eye contact, refusing to look her in the eyes.

"Yes, I am!" She pleaded, leaping towards him with her mermaid tail, rushing in to kiss him as hard as she could.

However before she could reach his lips, he stepped back and denied her.

"Oh, I get it!" Fuchsia exclaimed, "it's *you* who's not ready!" She couldn't help but let out a playful smirk. "Don't be so shy, my darling," she teased, "we can take things slow."

Becoming even angrier, the Captain persisted, "what are you talking about, you fish?"

"I'm *not* a fish!" Her jaw dropped, deeply offended.

"Truthfully, I was only trying to prevent you from becoming a queen. Now, leave!"

"So, you lied about being in love with me?"

"Yeah."

"Psh! You stopped me from being queen because you *cared*. Otherwise, what's the point? I can always just swim back home and be queen again. There's your loophole."

"Not anymore!" He struck his hand out and zapped her, a painless twinge flowed through her body, causing her tail to transform back into human legs, and her pink hair back to brown. The same white dress covered her body.

"Ahh!" She squealed.

"Good luck swimming back home *now*," he cruelly teased in the most immature manner. It was like he had become a totally different person! A child!

"Ugh!" Fuchsia stomped her feet, "fine!"

Jumping off of the boat, Fuchsia sank deep into the water, falling deeper... deeper... and deeper... until she swiftly floated back up for air -- and suddenly she found herself washed up on the shore. She was back on the sand in that little beach town, called "Oceana Paradise."

The weather calmed down, as the clouds graciously cleared away, revealing the glowing full moon. Although, it was getting darker, which meant she would have to find shelter soon.

It didn't matter to her that her mermaid powers were gone again. Just a few minutes of being queen made her realize that it certainly wasn't the life for her. Having everybody sucking up to her, while completely ignoring her plans to make a difference in the world, simply seemed like a life of misery.

Still in shock over what had just happened, Fuchsia blocked it out of her mind -- there was no time to think. Now she was in survival mode.

Fuchsia knew exactly where she wanted to go. She marched through the sand in her flip-flops and made her way back to the boardwalk. The town was lively, with salsa music playing in the background. The smell of oil filled her nose, mixed with the smell of the salty air, and she smiled. She realized that she missed it here.

There it was -- that glowing sign that read "PSYCHIC." Opening the door and taking a step inside, she saw Madame sitting there on her throne.

"Hello," Fuchsia greeted.

"Hello, young mermaid," Madame greeted back, clearly remembering their prior encounter.

"I need a job," she blurted out, "I wanna work here."

Madame was without words.

"You were right before, I have to work for what I want -- I cannot simply expect everything to come to me without the effort."

"Hmm," Madame silently nodded, letting her continue to speak.

"My intuition is very strong. It needs some work, but I really feel like I could learn a lot from you. I want to work here and live in this little beach town. I want to become a psychic. This is how I can help the humans."

"So you want to become a psychic?" Madame raised an eyebrow.

"Yes! Please! I promise you, I have what it takes!" She persuaded.

"Hmm…" the psychic pondered, "this is really only a one-woman business…"

"I understand," Fuchsia nodded, "I used to be an actress and I only did one-woman shows. So I know how it feels to desire working alone. However, I'm learning now that by accepting help and assistance, so much more can be accomplished."

Madame looked at her with hesitance.

"We could take double the customers!" Fuchsia proposed, "I could help with cleaning!"

"It does make me very happy to teach others and watch them grow…" she considered with caution.

"I beg of you!" Fuchsia clasped her hands together in prayer.

"Alright," Madame softened.

"Yes!" Fuchsia relieved with a deep sigh.

Madame ordered, "you'll work below minimum wage, under the table. It'll be just enough to keep you fed and clean. You'll start off as my janitor, spending your days scrubbing the floor, dusting the walls, wiping down the furniture, and so on. I want this place to look sparkly."

"It *could* use a little work," Fuchsia muttered, noticing cobwebs in the corner.

"And then, only once you have proven yourself, will you begin to learn the practice of being a psychic."

"Okay," Fuchsia agreed.

"So it's settled."

"Just one more thing..."

"What more could you want, child!?" Madame cried out.

"Uh..." Fuchsia hesitated, "a place to live?"

Madame's face went blank.

"I notice you have an upstairs..."

"I'll let you stay here, for now," Madame sighed, "but that means I want you on the clock for as long as you're awake. Unless you're eating or sleeping, you better be cleaning. Understood?"

"Yes!" Fuchsia exclaimed with joy, "just one more little teeny, tiny thing," she said in her sweetest voice possible.

"*What!?*"

"Can you teach me how to clean?"

With an eye roll, Madame agreed, "most certainly. Now let me add that I wouldn't do this for anyone else. I can read your energy, and I know you can be trusted, and you do have potential."

Fuchsia smiled widely.

Madame continued, "the only issue I see here is that you have a lot of impatience. You also have the tendency to be sassy every now and then, especially with that big ego of yours. So humble yourself, and you should be just fine."

"Yes, Miss Madame," Fuchsia stood up straight, attempting to prove her gratitude.

It was true, if Madame hadn't accepted her request, she would've been forced to go crying back to Mother Mermaid -- who would've sent her back to the ocean as queen again.

And then Fuchsia gulped. The thought of Mother Mermaid made her feel sick. Surely, she must've been disappointed that she ran away from her so-called destiny. But Fuchsia felt deep inside her heart that it was not in her destiny to be worshipped, but instead, to help the poor humans.

That night, Fuchsia was ecstatic to tuck herself into bed in her very own little room. The bed was so warm and cozy underneath the covers. She gave her achy legs a nice massage. With the window cracked, the soothing sound of crashing waves put her right to sleep.

At 12:00 AM sharp, her eyes burst wide open. Suddenly, Fuchsia was overcome with an intense urge to run outside. Following her instincts, she tiptoed downstairs and out onto the boardwalk. She lifted her head to look at the sky.

The stars seemed to be spelling out a distinct message. She squinted a little harder until she made out the words, "NOT READY!"

Both baffled and amazed, Fuchsia's sleepy head had no idea what to make of it. The Captain? Mother Mermaid? And so, she swiftly returned back to bed.

XV. MADAME'S PSYCHIC IN TRAINING

The following morning, Fuchsia groggily rubbed her eyes. Remembering what the stars had told her last night, she couldn't fully decipher whether it had been a dream or real life.

Since it was daytime, she could fully observe and appreciate her new bedroom. There was a lot going on compared to her old home, which was simply a cave full of rocks, surrounded by blue. Now, Fuchsia stood on a yarn carpet consisting of so many colors -- red, yellow, orange, green, dark blue, light blue. Her twin bed was just as colorful.

Mistakenly opening the closet door, which she confused for the bedroom door, her eyes widened when she found hangers full of dresses. All the dresses were even more colorful than the bedroom itself -- there was silver, gold, purple, brown... she paused when she found a hot pink, flowy sundress.

"Pink!" She shrieked in admiration, "just what my hair used to be..." she sighed, glancing over at her brown-haired self in the mirror. She thought out loud with a pout, "it wasn't such a shame that the Captain took away my tail and gave me legs, but why did he have to revoke my pink hair!?"

After blurting out the words, a sense of dread fell upon her. She was trying to avoid thinking about the Captain at all costs.

Shaking herself out of it, Fuchsia put the hot pink dress back into the closet and made her way downstairs where she found Madame.

"Good morning, Madame," Fuchsia politely greeted, "thank you again, so much, for this wonderful opportunity," she clasped her hands in prayer.

"You're welcome," she said, handing her a granola bar, "there's some snacks available for you in the back room. Once you start working, you'll have some money to go out on the boardwalk and buy yourself a fresh meal."

"Oh, thank you!" Fuchsia exclaimed.

"Now," Madame instructed, "I have closed the shop today, so I can teach you how to clean. That way we can cover all the basics without interruption. If you do well, I'll give you some starting cash. From then on, you'll get paid once a week, every Friday. Understood?"

"Yes, ma'am," Fuchsia nodded.

"Remember -- right now, you're my cleaner, and that is all. You may listen to the readings with my customers, you may watch from a distance -- but only while you are cleaning at the same time. Do not ask me to give you a psychic reading, and most importantly, do not ask to give a psychic reading yourself. These tools I use -- my crystal ball, my tarot cards, my runes, and so forth -- they are not toys, you hear me?"

"I understand," Fuchsia assured.

"Lovely," Madame smiled, "with patience and persistence, I think this could work out well."

"I won't let you down!" Fuchsia promised with glistening eyes.

And so, for the rest of the day, Madame taught Fuchsia all about cleaning. She learned how to use a vacuum, how to use a mop and bucket, how to spray, how to scrub, and so on. They started out in the main area -- the entrance area where the psychic readings are conducted. And then, they moved beyond the curtain, into a private corner that led into a miniscule kitchen. It had a mini fridge, a small table with one chair, and a stove.

Heading upstairs, Fuchsia peaked into Madame's bedroom, which was just as small as hers. Gravitating towards her new closet, Fuchsia questioned, "where did all these beautiful dresses come from?"

"Ah," Madame chuckled, "those are my vintage dresses from my golden years -- they're ancient!"

"They're so beautiful!" Fuchsia gushed.

"I almost forgot about these," Madame sighed, running her hands through the dresses with nostalgia, "this could be your new wardrobe, if you like them so much."

"Really? I would love that!" Fuchsia cheered, "it looks like you used to be the same exact size as me," she pulled on the dress's waistline.

"Yeah, *used to,*" Madame laughed, "brings back memories."

"Madame, do you mind if I ask how old you were when you became a psychic?"

She answered, "I have been psychic my whole life. But I began to study the esoteric arts when I was around nineteen or so."

"That's how old *I* am!"

Fuchsia could see herself in Madame, like she was her future. They were two free-spirited and independent women. The sense of trust and support she felt around this woman she hardly knew was unbelievable. She could see that Madame cared for her and wanted to nurture her -- not in a way that would spoil her, but a way that would genuinely help her grow.

It was a completely different energy than what she was used to with her sisters. With her sisters, they were always looking out for her -- especially Amber and Turquoise, the eldest ones. However, they never provided the discipline that she needed. Rather, they let her get away with anything -- and that's because life as a mermaid came with no consequences.

In contrast, life as a human was *full* of consequences. Fuchsia could see that there was no surviving without money, and there was no money without work. In the human world, she would have to work like never before -- the thought was both terrifying and exhilarating at the same time. Although she understood that work was painful, she also knew that work created progress -- something that no amount of pleasure could ever bring.

Progress was Fuchsia's escape from the feeling of swimming in circles all day. It was the concept that would lead her from point A to point B, rather than endlessly circling the same exact point for an entire lifetime. Progress was her key to finding fulfillment, filling that gaping hole inside of her, reaching a higher level of consciousness.

Towards the end of the day, as the sun was sinking lower to the ground, Madame offered, "here's some money for dinner -- you earned it."

Fuchsia thanked her, "oh, thank you kindly! Did I do a good job today?"

"You did fantastic. Keep it up. Now go enjoy yourself with something nice from the boardwalk, take a rest, and I'll see you first thing tomorrow morning."

Venturing onto the boardwalk, all by herself, Fuchsia's heart was racing. The fun salsa music was playing again, and it made her dance a little bit. Once again, there were crowds of all different groups of people. Instead of begging for company like she once did before, Fuchsia pleasantly decided to enjoy her own company.

As she was waiting in line for food at a hamburger stand, a kind stranger walked past her saying, "I like your dress -- it's so cute!"

Fuchsia was wearing one of Madame's -- the hot pink one that had reminded her of her original hair color.

"Thank you!" Fuchsia smiled, "that's so sweet of you to say."

Fuchsia was no stranger to compliments -- back in the ocean from her adoring merpeople fans -- but to receive one from a random human was astounding.

Sitting down on a bench that faced the ocean, Fuchsia enjoyed her burger and fries. It was perhaps one of the most delicious meals she'd ever consumed -- because she had *worked* for it. There was a better taste to it, and that didn't necessarily come from the satiating grease, but the labor of her own efforts.

Countless distractions of the human world kept her mind from trailing off towards the Captain. But now that she was finishing up her dinner, comfortably adjusting to her new surroundings, unwanted thoughts were peering through.

The scene from yesterday -- the total shipwreck -- replayed through her head like a broken film. Trying to figure out what happened, all she knew was that fear surely had something to do with it. She was nervous, he was nervous, and then all of the nervousness completely escalated. The Captain couldn't maintain control, so he took back control by pushing his mermaid away.

Fuchsia thought of that message written in the stars -- "NOT READY." She pondered -- *Am I not ready for the Captain? Is the Captain not ready for me? Am I not ready for my destiny?*

Remembering Madame's words from when she originally had her fortune read, she recalled what she had told her about destiny -- that destiny is reserved for those who are brave enough to choose it.

She inferred that the Captain was not quite brave enough for her and that was why he kicked her off of his ship. Alongside, she inferred that she herself was not quite brave enough for the Captain. Being a mermaid her whole life, she was too accustomed to always getting her way, to everything being handed to her, to never having to work for anything. She was used to constant pleasure without any pain, actions without consequences, a comfort bubble that could never pop.

Looking back, Fuchsia thought about how before the mermaid ball, she used to simply sit there, looking pretty on her rock, while the Captain sailed by. She never waved to him or called him over. Rather, she merely *expected* him to come back to her -- even though she was the first one to pull away when she denied him after their first encounter.

Returning to her new home, Fuchsia was ecstatic to fall asleep in her soft and cozy bed. In merely the span of twenty-four hours, she was already feeling so much braver. She was conquering the human world!

As badly as she wanted to despise the Captain, she could not escape from the truth -- she was absolutely desperate for his love. With faith, she believed that this was certainly not the end of this love story, that he would be back somehow. And this time, her fears would be completely conquered.

The following day, Fuchsia worked as hard as she possibly could. Using all of her efforts, she managed to make the entire home spotless. Meanwhile, she picked up very closely and carefully on the psychic readings that Madame conducted.

The day after, Fuchsia was hopeful for her first lesson.

"So," she began, "I cleaned basically everything there is to clean...."

"Good," Madame nodded, "keep on going."

"*More?*" Fuchsia nearly whimpered.

"Yes, more," Madame ordered.

And so, for the rest of the week, Fuchsia kept on cleaning. She got into every single corner and crevice that she could find. She moved all the furniture around. She wouldn't stop until her shirt was soaked with sweat.

"How's it look?" she asked.

"Very nice," Madame replied.

"So..." Fuchsia so badly wanted to ask about her psychic lessons, however, she tried as much as she could to hold back, knowing it would only anger Madame.

"Keep going."

For the next few weeks, Fuchsia did all she could in her power to resist asking Madame to finally teach her how to be a psychic. Instead, she paid extra attention to her customers. From afar, she was able to memorize the meanings of the tarot cards, as well as the meanings of the lines on people's hands. Under her bed, she found a box of books about fortune telling, and would read from them every night.

As much as she tried to resist it, Fuchsia often thought about the Captain. And when she did, there was anger. She used that vexation to scrub with extreme force. It was a therapeutic way of dealing with all that pent up energy.

Time continued passing, and she continued working diligently, going above and beyond to prove to Madame that she was worth it. She cleaned as hard as she could, then cleaned some more, and then cleaned even more.

As excruciating as it was, she continued to persevere. But one day, Fuchsia felt herself cracking. She couldn't stand it anymore.

"Madame," Fuchsia pleaded after a long, hot, sweaty day of work, "may I please..." she panted, "please... PLEASE..."

"Not yet," Madame immediately answered.

"Just *touch* one of the tarot cards?"

"Nope."

"Just take a *quick peek* into the crystal ball?"

"Nope."

"Just…" she moaned, "just… just…"

"Nope, nope, nope," Madame shook her head.

"*GAHHH!*" exasperated, Fuchsia threw her hands in the air.

"If you were as psychic as you believe," Madame softly said, "you would not continue asking me. You will know when you're ready."

Suddenly, just as Fuchsia was about to storm out the door in total frustration, her eyes lit up as she watched a new customer walk through the door — it was Zale!

"Zale?" Fuchsia gasped.

"Fuchsia," he smiled.

Madame raised an eyebrow.

"I had a feeling I'd find you here…" Zale said.

Fuchsia had been hoping to avoid him, but after so many weeks of nonstop cleaning and doing whatever Madame commanded, he was exactly who she wanted to see.

"Save me!" Fuchsia cried out, "I've never worked this hard in my life, this is absolutely exhausting!"

"Oh, you work here now?"

"Yes!"

"Work is tiring, get used to it," he sarcastically commented.

"Honey, you've been doing well," Madame admitted, "you deserve a break. Why don't you take lunch with your friend here?"

"Oh my goodness!" Fuchsia clasped her hands in prayer, "a break would be delightful!" She cheered.

"Wow," Zale raised his eyebrows, impressed, "sounds like you've been dedicated, I'm proud of you."

"Yeah, see?" Fuchsia back-sassed, "you thought I couldn't handle having a job!"

"When did I ever say that!?" Zale furrowed his eyebrows in absolute puzzlement.

"Go on, children," Madame shooed them away.

Taking in a deep breath of freedom, Fuchsia inhaled the fresh air with satisfaction, as her and Zale stepped out on the boardwalk.

Fuchsia bursted out, "all I've been doing, the past few weeks, or maybe even longer, I don't know, I've lost track of time, is work, work, work, sleep, work, sleep, work, work, work, sleep, work, sleep, work, work…"

"Please, slow down," he urged.

"This is not what mermaids do, I mean, we just laugh and play all day and occasionally go spearfishing for food, but this is just madness," speaking so fast almost tripping over her words, "I can't do it. I can't handle it. I gotta get out of here. But the Captain, he's supposed to come back. I think. I don't know. I can't go back to mermaid life, I can't. But maybe I'm supposed to. I don't know. Oh my God–"

"Take a breath."

Fuchsia paused for a moment to breathe.

"Let's go get a snack or something, have some fun," he suggested.

"Sure," she agreed.

Fuchsia noticed that Zale seemed much more distant and serious than the last time they had spoken.

The two of them got strawberry lemonade and crispy boardwalk fries, and then sat down to eat on a bench table in the sand.

"How are you?" Zale inquired with genuine concern, "have you been eating?" He noticed her gobbling down her fries as if she hadn't consumed anything in weeks.

"Yes, Madame pays for my meals," Fuchsia explained, "I've been having lots of fries, can't get enough of them. Also a lot of fish, shrimp, and lobster. Reminds me of home, but way, way greasier. Man, you guys love your oil and butter. You can't even taste the actual animal. It's tasty, but it sure makes my tummy hurt."

Zale chuckled, and let her continue to ramble.

"I'm trying new stuff too, like..." Fuchsia thought for a moment, combing through her memory, "pizza! Pasta! Ice cream!" Her face lit up.

"And crepes?" He teased.

"Lots, and lots, of crepes!" She exclaimed with joy.

He chuckled again.

"Mmm," she moaned.

"I was gonna say," he commented, "the way you eat, it looks like you've been starving."

"This is just how I eat," Fuchsia defended herself, "is there something wrong?"

"No, no!" Zale shook his head, "you must really enjoy it; it's cute," he giggled.

"Well, how would *you* eat if you hadn't tasted grease like this your whole life?" Fuchsia continued.

"It's simply an observation," Zale assured, "you don't have to bark back like that."

"Hmph."

"Are you a little belligerent, Fuch?" Zale teased jokingly.

"Who, me?" Fuchsia raised her eyebrows, "never! I'm a very peaceful person," she stated confidently.

"Okay," Zale chuckled.

Letting her finish the meal, Zale kept silent as he watched Fuchsia chow down in admiration.

"I came here to tell you something," Zale confessed. He looked around to double check that no one else was in sight. They were in a far, secluded area.

Sensing the sudden seriousness in his voice, Fuchsia's heart sank.

Scotching herself back for more space, she replied with anxiety, "you're making me nervous... what is it?"

He hesitated, stuck in his head, staring straight ahead.

"Is this going to be about how you have a crush on me, again?" She assumed.

He looked back at her, into her eyes, "I can tell that you feel something."

"No," she denied in aggravation, "I don't. Can't we just have fun together without you bringing this up every single time?"

"Are you sure?" He raised an eyebrow.

"Yes!" She nearly screamed.

"One more question..." he slyly added.

"What!?" She threw her hands in the air.

"Ever seen someone shapeshift?"

"*Shapeshift?* Like, change bodies? Change form?" She squinted.

And then, Fuchsia widened her eyes as she witnessed Zale's body glitch, like she was inside of a video game, and morph into a completely different person.

He wasn't Zale anymore. Who was it!? Could it actually be...!?

"It's me," he said, "I'm the Captain."

"Wh-what?" She stuttered in shock.

"It's been me this whole time."

"Zale?"

"There is no 'Zale,' he's fictitious. I made him up."

Overcome with countless conflicting emotions, she had no idea what to say, let alone what to think.

"Well?" The Captain stared at her, desperate for a reaction. But she was frozen.

"Who *else* have you been?" She finally responded, "that magical girl, Rainbow... that was also you?"

"Yes," he admitted.

"And who else? Madame, the psychic? That kind stranger, Shayla? And what about Zale's friends, were you all of them, too?"

"No," he explained, "just Zale... and Rainbow. I can't be two people at once... I'm not *that* gifted," he half-joked.

"I'm just a little confused... just a bit..." she could barely manage to get out the words.

"Fuchsia, we've settled that you don't like me. You made that very clear. So stop chasing after this 'captain' figure, cause it's not me. You only want what you can't have."

"Hey!" She shouted back in defense, "that is so not fair! I thought you were someone else!"

"Exactly," he nodded.

"Wait! Why won't you give me a chance? It's like you keep setting me up for failure."

"I know the ending of this story. You're hooked on me until you actually get to know me. Once you learn who I am, you'll run," he groaned in disdain.

"Love at first sight!" She exclaimed, "I already know you, I know your soul!"

"You know a fantasy, and that's all."

"Why won't you let your guard down?"

"I've already said enough. It's time to go now."

"No!" She begged, "we were just having such a great time together! Let's go swimming! Let's get more food! Let's talk! Anything!"

"I've already made my point."

"What point!? That you won't even give me a fair chance? You'd rather merely assume that I don't truly love you?"

The Captain paused for a moment to gather his thoughts.

And finally, he added, "go back to all your boyfriends."

"Oh, is *that* what this is actually about? Too many boys in my life? You know, I've left them all behind for you."

"I saw all of them rushing towards you back in the ocean, when you were queen. They were all drooling over you."

"You saw all that? How?" Fuchsia wondered how much of her he saw without her realizing it. She asked herself, *could he see me working my butt off these past few weeks?*

"I can't believe I stopped you from being queen. If I hadn't said anything at all, you'd be back in the ocean, ruling as queen, making plans for world peace, living happily ever after with your king."

"That's not true!" Fuchsia defended, "you were warning me -- and you were right! Look, I used to be an actress..."

"If I had a piece of gold for every time you said, '*I used to be an actress*,'" he sarcastically mocked.

"Oh, just listen!" She rolled her eyes, "I used to be an actress, I used to be famous and beautiful."

"What are you talking about? You're still beautiful."

"No," Fuchsia reinforced, "I've got boring-brown hair, wiggly legs with these weird dimples, dull skin, and now I'm getting these ugly red dots all over my chin!"

"Those are pimples," he giggled.

Fuchsia growled at him with her fangs.

"But you make them look beautiful," he added.

"Ugh, what was I saying?"

"You were an actress..."

"Oh, right. I had that constant attention, those adoring fans, and that sense of worship long before I was ever 'queen' for a day. It was just on a much, much smaller scale. And all of that is exactly why I wanted to get away from my old life. I was living on auto-pilot with no sense of direction. I craved a thrill -- not just a quick high with a speedy comedown, but a sense of traveling outside of my comfort zone and never coming back! A whirlwind romance that would sweep me away from superficiality and make me feel something real," she let out a deep breath.

"I'm not sure if I can give you all of that," he sighed.

"Of course you can! You have challenged me more than anyone else I've ever known! You're the reason I'm living here -- I'm one of the humans -- it's the craziest and bravest thing I've ever done!"

"I know you'll find your perfect king someday."

"It's *you*, my Captain!" Fuchsia passionately urged.

"It's time for me to go."

"No, it's not! I'm begging you to stay, what more else do you want!?"

"Goodbye."

"No, wait!"

"Have a nice life."

"Can I just ask one thing?"

"... What?"

"Why 'Zale'? Is that code for something?"

He explained, "I passed this store, with all these diamonds. It's what humans give each other when they get married. And I thought of you."

"That's so sweet," she gushed, "you wanna marry me? See, you *do* really love me," she persuaded.

"Let it be," he said, before disappearing into thin air.

"No!" She cried out in panic, "wait!"

But he was gone -- nowhere in sight.

"Captain, come back!" She yelled to the sea, "you don't believe in me! You really don't believe in me!"

She stood still for a second, giving him a chance to reappear.

And then finally, with defeat, she quickly said, "I believe in myself, and that's enough."

XVI. YEARNING
FOR DESTINY

Several more months passed, and how agonizing that time was...

Fuchsia returned back to work and attempted to stay strong. It was time to move past this perplexing man, and focus on her new adventure -- despite the small part of her that desperately clung onto hope. Each time a customer came into the shop, she secretly prayed it was the Captain in disguise. But it never was.

She spent her days cleaning, eating, more cleaning, sleeping, and then back to cleaning again. Madame *still* refused to let her learn about becoming a psychic.

Fuchsia intently observed every time Madame conducted a reading. At this point, she already felt completely capable. She had now memorized all the meanings of the tarot cards, all the lines of the palm, and all the other secrets of being a psychic. Whenever she had free time, which was rare, she went into meditation so deep that it felt like traveling through space. All of these things she learned simply from watching. Now, if only, Madame would actually teach her directly.

Although she never saw the Captain anymore, it was impossible to get him off her mind. Every single night she had a vivid dream where she saw him. Yet in these dreams, they never touched, they only shared a quick glance. Even in her wildest fantasies, he was merely a distant blimp.

Some nights, she woke up and saw the stars spell out messages for her, just as they did that first night. Often they said quick things such as "*My mermaid*" or "*watching, waiting.*" She didn't understand where these messages came from or what they meant, but she certainly questioned why the Captain couldn't come back to her if he was still thinking of her. Then again, perhaps these messages had nothing to do with him, and were actually coming straight from her subconscious mind.

Fuchsia understood that at any moment, she could return home to her ocean, where she once belonged. All she had to do was beg to Mother Mermaid and obey her plan. However, this was her new home now. The thought of learning how to help and heal the humans someday with her intuitive ability gave her much excitement and hope -- it was her ultimate destiny. The merpeople couldn't understand this.

One day, a customer came in, and all of a sudden as she was sweeping, Fuchsia fell to the ground, randomly losing balance. Placing her hand on her heart, she felt an unsettling heaviness in her chest. She was already aching over the Captain, but in this moment, she felt a stabbing pain like never before.

"Are you okay?" The woman asked, horrified!

Bug-eyed, Fuchsia examined this woman's aura -- black, with swirls of grey, like a raging storm cloud surrounding her.

"Uh..." Fuchsia replied slowly lifting herself off the floor, "are... are *you* okay?" She had never felt so much pain in a human's aura before.

"My dear, welcome!" Madame popped out from behind the curtain, "sorry about that -- how can I help you? May I offer you a reading?"

"Please," she sighed, "I need help, immediately."

"Sit down," Madame instructed, sitting with her at the table.

Fuchsia couldn't help but continue staring at this woman. She knew it wasn't the Captain, she was sure of it. The reason why she was so struck was because this woman was in such intense emotional agony that it was taking over. Her gloomy vibes were spreading throughout the room, painting the entire shop grey -- yet Madame managed to keep a clear bubble around herself, protecting her own energy field.

Fuchsia had seen plenty of auras, many sad ones, but nothing as strong and contagious as this one. Frozen, standing there still with her broom in hand, her eyes were glued to Madame and her client.

"What's your name?" asked Madame.

"Bethany," she answered, handing over a fist full of cash.

Madame double-counted the money, and with a nod, shoved it in her register. Next, shuffling her cards, Madame casually asked, "alright Bethany, tell me what's going on, my darling."

Instantly bursting into tears, Bethany whimpered, "my boyfriend left me a few days ago. We were living together. I woke up one day -- all his stuff was gone. I called a million times -- no answer. Finally, he picks up and tells me he's been cheating on me for months with another woman! He said he left me for her, told me to never talk to him again, and then he blocked my number! We were dating for two years!"

Jaw dropping to the floor, Fuchsia shook her head in denial, "are you serious!?" She heavily empathized.

Madame, clearing her throat, gave Fuchsia the side-eye, and then continued, "I see, I see," laying three cards down on the table.

Out they popped -- *The Tower. Death. Three of swords.*

Fuchsia's eyes grew even wider, nearly popping out of her sockets now.

"Aha," Madame calmly nodded.

"What's that one mean?" Bethany pointed to the "three of swords," an image of a heart with three swords stabbed in it.

"Honey, this looks bad," Madame explained, "I'm seeing an affair, sudden shock, your whole life changing and flipping upside-down."

"Exactly!" Bethany nodded, "so please, tell me, will he come back to me?"

"Let me see your hand." Observing her client's palm for a minute, Madame discovered, "you have a lot of childhood wounds that need healing. This healing can't be done while you're in a relationship and giving so much of yourself to someone else. I would advise you to stay single and work on these inner issues if you want to clear your karma and find a better partner in the future. This traumatic breakup is a blessing in disguise."

"But," Bethany refused, "I don't want anyone else! You really can't see us getting back together? Tell me, how do I make him come back to me? How!?"

"I can't see that happening," Madame explained, "this is not meant to be."

"He's never coming back?" Bethany attempted to swallow, staring like a deer caught in headlights. "There has to be a way to bring him back. Don't you have any advice?"

"My dear, I don't want you wasting your breath on this connection anymore. There's no potential at all."

"This new girl... does she make him happy?"

Gazing into her crystal ball, Madame answered, "yes, he's happy..." and then paused, "for now. I don't see it lasting, but I see them together for a while, possibly getting engaged. But they won't make it past that."

Bowing her head in her face in total despair, all Bethany heard was, "*he's happy?* She really makes him happy?" More tears.

"Madame," Fuchsia couldn't help but cut in, "surely you must have some advice, or something, that can bring these two back together. Even temporarily."

"Forever!" Bethany panicked, "I want us to last forever! I don't want to get back together just to fall apart again!"

"Okay!" Fuchsia appeased, trying to calm her down, "there has to be something she can do!"

"Excuse me, Fuchsia," Madame said, rather annoyed, "I believe the bathroom needs more scrubbing."

Caught off guard, she sassed back, "uh, I believe I scrubbed it decently... for hours."

"You better get back to your job before you don't have one anymore!" Madame exclaimed.

Frustrated, Fuchsia stormed behind the curtain where she could still eavesdrop on the conversation.

Leaning in, she could hear Madame continue, "sweetie, this relationship is done for good. Whatever you do to win him back won't last. And if you force him to stay with you, you'll both end up miserable."

"I don't care!" Bethany said out of breath, "I don't care if I'm miserable! I want him, and no one else! I'd rather be miserable with him than happy with anybody else!"

"This is how I see it."

"I can't believe this."

"For extra charge, I can tell you about your next lover. He looks quite handsome already," Madame half-smiled, continuing to gaze into her crystal ball.

"No," Bethany sighed, "no, thanks." And with that, she politely exited.

"Come again soon!" Madame called out.

And now that it sounded safe to return, Fuchsia opened the curtain and walked herself back into the main room.

No longer grey, the air was clear again. Bethany's melancholy energy was gone. For good measure, Madame lit a wand of sage and waved it around.

"How could you?" Fuchsia struck.

"You have got a lot of nerve, young child," Madame sighed in anger.

"Me!?"

"That was extremely unprofessional of you, to butt into a reading like that."

"Who cares about professionalism, when that girl was literally dying on the inside!? Don't you feel bad!?"

"Of course I feel bad! But it's not my job to make her feel better. I get paid to see the future. I'm not a doctor or psychologist -- it would be vastly irresponsible of me to claim myself as one. I'm just the messenger between worlds."

"I'm only saying, you could've been a little nicer, that's all."

"I was very polite."

"You didn't have to be so blunt. You could've bent the truth a little, maybe tell her there's a slight chance he'll come back."

"That would be lying."

"Ugh!" Fuchsia huffed. She realized the argument was over, suddenly remembering all those times others accused her of being too blunt, when all she ever intended was honesty. Yet still, to see someone in so much pain get knocked down even further, was unforgivably heartbreaking. And then she added, "I just feel so horrible for that poor girl, no one deserves that."

"Now, do you see?" Madame told her, "this is why you're not ready to be a psychic."

"What do you mean, why?"

"You have no defense. You have no boundaries. You absorb people's energies like a sponge. Yes, it's important to observe and comprehend your client's energy, but there must be a line between you two."

Fuchsia squinted her eyes in skepticism, trying to understand.

Madame continued, "it's a gift to see auras, but a terrible curse to feel them. These clients come in, all of them are hurting. If you were to give them psychic readings, you'd be sick by the end of the day, you'd become so drained that you'd lose all your strength."

"How do I protect myself?"

"It takes a vast amount of practice... you can start with imagining a protective bubble around yourself."

"Okay," Fuchsia nodded in determination, "I'll work on it."

"You can't just tell people what they want to hear in order to make them happy. People come to me for the truth, so the truth you shall deliver."

"I guess I see your point," Fuchsia reluctantly shrugged.

"I see the future, but I'm no magician. I can't just make someone feel better, although I believe that becoming more aware of yourself and what your future holds is the first step to healing. I may not heal; I give others the opportunity to heal themselves. It's a choice one person must make on their own. I showed that woman, Bethany, how moving on will benefit her -- but I cannot force her to move on, that's a choice she must make herself when she's ready."

In silence, Fuchsia pondered hard about what Madame had taught her. Perhaps she was right, perhaps fortune-telling was a heavy responsibility that she was not prepared for.

Fuchsia wondered, "what does a healer do?"

Madame answered, "well, a healer can be a doctor who prescribes medicine. Rather, a *psychic* healer works directly with energy. They can cure someone through touch or even thought. But that is a rare gift -- only saints are healers."

Fuchsia nodded, imagining herself to be a psychic healer. She could cure people of their broken hearts and possibly save the human race. Then maybe, if all the humans were healed, they could coexist openly with the mermaids and mermen in peace. There would be no war or exploitation.

More weeks passed, and Fuchsia continued attempting to shield herself from people's auras, to observe them without absorbing them. Yet it was becoming increasingly difficult to focus, as the Captain was protruding her mind even more strongly now.

Every time a customer would come in, she couldn't help but wonder -- *was it him? Was he shapeshifting, still?*

But no, none of them had strong enough energies to be him. She recalled, with Zale and Rainbow, that she felt drawn to them like magnets -- that's how she would know if someone was the Captain in disguise.

Walking along the boardwalk, aimlessly, she continued to wonder. Every face that passed her by — *could it be him? No, of course not...*

She stood at the edge of the pier, staring off into the distance. Every ship that sailed by — *the Captain? ...No.*

As her depression grew -- unexpectedly, so did her creativity. While cleaning for Madame in total boredom, her mind constantly drifting to the Captain, she began crafting poems.

Unable to fall asleep one night, she ran out to the boardwalk and sang her poem to the sea...

"Wandering soul, I've lost my way.
Deserting a life of fun and play.
Slaving myself now, day after day,
To call this my choice, is peculiar to say.
I was destined for more than the sea
Conquering hardship was meant for me.
I will accomplish something so great,
Unite my merpeople with the human race!
Yet I must confess, the hidden truth.
My Captain, I'm doing this all for you..."

Fuchsia ran back to her little home, the psychic shop. Before heading inside, she noticed a black cat cross her path.

"Aww!" She squealed with joy, "what a cute, fluffy creature you are!" Leaning down, she cautiously stuck out her hand, offering to pet it. The poor thing looked starving.

The scrawny kitten rushed towards Fuchsia and rubbed its head against her legs, letting her scratch behind its ears in joy.

"You are so adorable!" She gushed, hearing its loud purrs.

Taken aback, she reexamined the black cat and saw it no longer looked like a hungry stray, but nourished and healthy.

"Wait, what!?" Fuchsia panicked, "you looked about five pounds just two seconds ago!" She felt its full belly. "Have I healed you!?"

The cat winked at her, and then quickly ran away!

"N-no way..." she stuttered in disbelief, "Captain...?"

But the cat was running faster now, and out of sight by the time Fuchsia could stand back up on her feet.

"Captain!?" She screamed.

Waiting a moment, no response... so, she took herself inside and upstairs to bed. Searching outside the window, the magic cat was gone for good.

The next morning, Fuchsia woke up feeling terrible.

"You're sick," Madame determined, the moment she saw her.

"And good morning to you, too," Fuchsia furrowed her eyebrows, appalled, "that's no way to greet someone."

"I can't have you around my clients with this sickly energy, it's going to throw off all my readings," she panicked.

"I'm fine," Fuchsia, annoyed, placed her hand on her own forehead to check her temperature, adding, "just a bad mood, is all."

"You're spiritually sick," Madame urged. Flustered, she swiftly brewed a cup of herbal tea for Fuchsia, motioning her to sit down in a chair, as she placed several crystals on her lap. "Drink this, it will help you vomit."

"I don't need to vomit!" Fuchsia stubbornly replied, "I'm not nauseous or anything!"

"You have a lot of suppressed emotions that you need to vomit up," she demanded. Sitting down next to her, Madame said, "tell me what is wrong."

"I dunno," Fuchsia said, "working hard, trying to shield my energy field, but I guess that's not working."

"Aha!" Madame lit up, "you've blocked out everyone else's emotions, so now you can finally face your *own*!"

"My *own* emotions?"

"Yes, they're coming to the surface for detox and release."

Slouching further down into her chair, Fuchsia sighed, "I'm flooded with thoughts that I've been constantly trying to get away from."

"So, set them free. Tell me what these thoughts are."

"It's..." she looked down, "it's the Captain. I always feel like he's thinking of me, or watching me, and yet he refuses to be with me. It takes him so much just to talk to me, and then he runs away. He's haunting me!" She threw her arms in the air. "And then I worry it's all in my head."

Madame silently nodded, giving her space to speak more.

So, Fuchsia continued, "you said we would end up together, but I just can't see that happening at this point. Was it really true, your prediction?"

Madame answered, "you know I never tell people what they want to hear, I tell people the truth."

"But I don't understand. I've lost all hope. Could it be that your prediction changed?"

"As I've explained before, nothing is set in stone -- not even destiny."

"Did I screw it up, then?"

"Are you still following your heart?"

"I am..." Fuchsia paused, "at least, I *think* I am... how do I know for sure?"

"Destiny is not easy or effortless."

"I made the choice to work for you and learn from you... as discouraging as it has been, might I add... and at any moment, I could return home to my village where they promised to make me queen. And that would be the easiest, most effortless life ever... which is why I knew it wasn't for me."

"There you go."

"I try to tell myself that I'm doing this for mankind, for the mermaids and the mermen, for world peace. But to be totally honest, I'm not a savior or a saint. I don't have healing powers, as much as I wish I did. Deep down, I just want to run away with the Captain and forget about everyone else... as selfish as it sounds."

"Oh, my love, you don't have to be everyone's hero. You can be one person's hero, and that is enough. Most people don't get to be anyone's hero."

With a sigh of relief, Fuchsia admitted, "it feels good to get that off of my chest."

"You look better already. Stay put while I make you another cup of tea." Madame stood up and turned on her kettle, sprinkling more herbs into the mug, followed by a splash of boiling water. She went on, "when two souls have been together for many lifetimes, each lifetime becomes increasingly difficult for them to reunite. Think of it as 'leveling up,' the evolution of your soul. Almost like a game, with each incarnation -- if you've passed your tests during the previous one -- your next life is a higher level with greater challenges. It is the more evolved soulmates who struggle the most to be together."

Speechless, Fuchsia took a moment to take it all in.

Still going, Madame explained, "and if this is your last level, then this is the hardest of them all. Souls who are strong enough to defeat the final level can break the cycle of reincarnation and reach Heaven together."

"Wow," she raised her eyebrows, "that's... that's... that's beautiful!"

"It's really simple -- you never give up hope. That's all."

"Madame, can I ask you a personal question?" Fuchsia inquired, "do you have a soulmate? Have you ever been in love?" She looked at her hand, noticing there was no wedding ring.

"Yes," Madame smiled. "My husband. We faced many, many tests together. It was no walk in the park; it was a battlefield."

"What happened?"

"He passed away many years ago. That's when I became a professional psychic and started this business, so I could still feel him with me every day. And I do."

"Oh, Madame, I am so sorry," Fuchsia sympathized, "you weren't always a professional psychic?"

"No, dear," she shook her head, "I had my own business before, I was always an entrepreneur woman. I made and sold jewelry. It was in this exact shop. And then after his passing, I sold our home and made this place my new home."

Fuchsia hesitated to ask, but was itching to know more, "do you think you'll ever remarry? Or find someone else?"

Sighing, she concluded, "no... I'm asked that more and more often, as time goes on. And I know people remarry all the time, and love is all around us, and some people are destined for that path, I completely understand. But personally, that's not my path."

"Hmm," Fuchsia stared at Madame's hand again, "what did your engagement ring look like?"

"I never wore one," she quickly shook her head, pulling out a beautiful gold necklace from under her dress, "I always preferred necklaces. We always did things differently, him and I."

"That's a beautiful necklace," Fuchsia gushed, "and children, did you ever have children?"

"No," she shook her head, "we never had children."

"Oh," Fuchsia nodded, feeling slightly uncomfortable now, as if she was breaking down a personal barrier of Madame's -- she was elusive and avoided revealing very much. "My apologies," she added, "I'm getting too personal.

"Not at all," Madame smiled, "it wasn't the path for us, or for me."

Fuchsia couldn't resist wondering, "you never had that childhood dream about falling in love and starting a family?"

"I did fall in love -- with my beloved husband. He is still with me now. And this psychic business I've created -- this is my baby, my legacy -- the whole family is here."

"You're right," Fuchsia beamed.

There was a strange sense of trust between the two of them. Fuchsia knew that Madame knew of her true mermaid identity, but it was hardly ever openly discussed. After all this time working for her, she never worried about her secret coming out. Fuchsia always suspected that Madame was more than human, with her incredibly accurate psychic abilities, but she couldn't put her finger on it. She pondered, "a mermaid, turned into a mortal, just like me? Or an alien, sent from outer space?" Whatever it was, she sadly figured there was no way of ever finding out.

Fuchsia snapped out of her haze when Madame abruptly exclaimed, "it's time to open the shop!" She opened the front door and turned the sign around from "sorry, we're closed!" to "come in, we're open!" And then, she said to Fuchsia, "looks like you're feeling much better, so I can do my readings properly. Yet just in case, go to bed and rest up. You deserve a day off."

Fuchsia was flabbergasted. She never had a day off, even weekends and holidays she was forced to work full shifts. Without question, she graciously nodded and ran upstairs to take a long nap.

After laying in bed all day, Fuchsia decided that she had become completely fed up with the Captain -- she *had* to find him, some-way, somehow.

XVII. PROPHETIC VISIONS

That evening, instead of heading to the boardwalk for dinner, Fuchsia headed straight towards the Sea Salt hotel.

Her heart was pounding. She had no idea what she was going to say to him, she just had to see him again. If he needed her to prove her love to him, then so be it!

Rushing inside, she was stopped again by the same hotel clerk from last time.

"Checking in?" She asked.

"No," Fuchsia explained, "I'm visiting my friend -- my boyfriend."

"What room number?"

"It's Zale -- room 207."

"I believe he checked out the other day," the woman scrolled through her computer.

"What?" Fuchsia lost her breath for a moment.

"Ah, yes," she confirmed, "yesterday at twelve o'clock."

"He's gone? That's impossible," she denied. "Can I double check, just in case?"

"It says here that the room is vacant. But sure, go ahead," the woman carelessly shrugged, and went back to reading her book.

Running upstairs, Fuchsia made her way to room 207 and saw that the door had been left wide open. There was no one there -- not a single trace of anything that'd been left behind. She searched in the drawers and under the two beds to see if he had left her any clues -- nothing!

Bursting into tears, Fuchsia grabbed a pillow and screamed into it. *He's gone,* she told herself, *it's over.*

After a few minutes of attempting to calm herself down, she made her way back to bed. She was too depressed to eat any dinner.

Laying in bed, struggling to fall asleep, Fuchsia heard rattling coming from out her window. She peeked out to see that the black cat had climbed up her fire escape. He pawed on the window. She cracked it open just enough for him to climb into her bed. Purring, she petted him softly.

"Who are you?" Fuchsia asked, "could you really be another form of the Captain -- or are you simply a cat?" She sighed, "I'm going crazy. Or course, you're just a cat."

Immediately, the cat jumped right back out the window and climbed down the fire escape.

"Hey!" Fuchsia called out, watching him run away, "get back here -- I need something to comfort me!"

She rushed downstairs, out the door, and found the cat running towards the beach, so she chased him. It was the middle of the night and no one else was around.

Before she could catch up to him, the cat was out of sight. So she looked up at the stars -- and that's when she saw another message spelled out -- "LOVE."

"*Love!?*" Fuchsia screamed out, "what is happening!? Where are these messages coming from!? Where are you, Captain!? If you really love me, then why are you gone!?"

Fuchsia couldn't stand it anymore. She needed answers immediately. Running back inside, she stared at Madame's desk with all her magical tools -- the tarot cards, the crystal ball, the runes, and so forth. Knowing Madame was fast asleep, this would be the perfect time to sneak in her own psychic reading.

Fuchsia sat down on the golden throne and stared into the crystal ball. She asked, "where is my Captain?"

Gazing deeper... and deeper... and deeper... the crystal ball remained clear. She couldn't see anything.

Frustrated, Fuchsia pulled a random tarot card from the deck, and it read, "The Moon" -- an image of wolves howling at the moon.

"None of this helps!" Fuchsia threw her arms up in exaltation, "I have no idea what I'm doing!"

Frustrated, she stormed off to bed.

The next morning, while Madame was sitting on her golden throne and sorting through her spiritual tools, Fuchsia slapped a twenty dollar bill on the table.

"It's all I can afford," she explained, "but please, I need a reading."

In skepticism, Madame commented, "something is off about the energy here -- did you rummage through my tools last night?"

"I can't lie to you," Fuchsia's face turned red, "I cracked, okay? I'm officially desperate. Go ahead, fire me."

"I admit that you've been working hard," Madame unexpectedly confessed, "I'm honestly impressed. Just swear to me that you'll never touch my tools without permission again."

"I promise."

Madame slid the twenty back towards Fuchsia, "I won't accept this."

"Please!" Fuchsia got down on her knees, "I'll work even harder, I'll skip my lunches, anything!"

"Fuchsia," Madame smirked, "this one's on the house."

"Huh?"

"You've earned it. Keep this twenty and get yourself a haircut. Your split ends are looking straggly."

"Uh, okay," Fuchsia was flabbergasted.

"Now, to your reading!" Madame excitedly cheered, as if she'd been looking forward to this moment.

Fuchsia sat herself down on the velvet couch as Madame gazed into her crystal ball. For a few seconds, Madame closed her eyes, taking in the energy, before returning to viewing her crystal.

"You want to know about the Captain and what he's up to."

"Yes," Fuchsia anxiously nodded and leaned forward.

"The Captain is a good man, but he is terribly closed. He has faced many betrayals in his lifetime which has caused him to become a hermit."

Fuchsia nodded again, and added, "he told me before that he was born a merman, that Mother Mermaid called upon him to be king. But he said he failed her test, that being king drove him mad, and so he faked his death to spend the rest of his life sailing the seas."

"I'm getting that, this was a test, but he did not fail. Mother Mermaid has been training him to take her place someday, as Father

Merman. She made him king to see how he would handle such a power -- if he would love the fame or despise it. She had to be sure that as Father Merman, he would not take advantage of his powerful influence."

"She wants him to be Father Merman? To rule with her?"

"No -- to take her place. Mother Mermaid has been sick for a while now. The merpeople species used to be much more spiritual. They used to spend their days praying for the humans, working behind the scenes to spread the message of peace and love. Yet since she's fallen ill in the past few hundred years, the merpeople have turned to alcohol and other distractions. Most of them even deny the existence of Mother Mermaid."

Fuchsia was silent, trying to absorb it all.

Madame continued, "and you didn't fail your test, either. I see you've been hiding from Mother Mermaid in shame since you denied being queen, and chose to run away with the Captain instead. She wants you to know that you passed your test -- you denied fame and worship because you saw how it overpowered your plan for your species, your plan to help the humans."

"Wait, really?" Fuchsia was astounded, "so I haven't betrayed her?"

"She can see all. She knew you would deny being queen, once you saw what it truly entailed -- she simply needed to prove it. And she knew that you would flee towards the Captain, that you would face another separation, and that you would come back to Oceana Paradise in order to find your own strength."

"Then why have I been suffering?"

"You haven't -- it's *growing pains*. This is what soul growth feels like. It's not very pleasurable."

"Why is she keeping me apart from the Captain?"

"She is doing her best to bring you two together. She wants you two to take her place as Mother Mermaid and Father Merman, to bring love back into the world."

"B-but why? How? I just..." Overwhelmed, Fuchsia had so many questions, but was lost for words.

"This is all I can tell you."

"Madame!" Fuchsia slammed her hands on the table, "you can't end it on a cliffhanger like that!"

"Sweetie, this is in your favor!" Madame urged, "if I reveal anything more, your head will surely explode! In fact, my own head is spinning dizzy. You have a grand destiny -- that's for sure."

"I'm still confused, though, I think I may be even *more* confused now..."

"Take some time to process what you've learned."

"What am I supposed to do, as the new Mother Mermaid?"

"If you keep on asking questions, you'll never leave space to hear the answers. Now silence your mouth, silence your thoughts, and wait."

Fuchsia sighed, agreeing that there was some wisdom in Madame's words. The rest of the day, as she cleaned the place, she could keep her lips zipped, but she couldn't shut off her darn mind.

Mother Mermaid has been testing me in order for me to take her place as the new Mother Mermaid? Alongside, she has also been testing the Captain for the past couple hundred years, in order to make him the new Father Merman? Also, what happened to the original 'Father Merman?' I never even knew there was such a thing!

At this point, Fuchsia was thinking so hard that she was staring into space, completely dissociating from her surroundings.

Goddess and God of the sea? Could that really be us? What does that mean? What would we do? Would the merpeople pray to us? Would we become all-knowing? Would we save the world!?

But wait... what would happen to Mother Mermaid? Why has she become sick? Is she dying? How is it possible for a goddess to die? Is that what happened to Father Merman, he died!?

The next thing she knew, it was already dinnertime, and Madame was closing up the shop for the night.

"Staying in or going out?" Madame asked.

At first, Fuchsia used to always go out on her own for dinner -- she was so curious and excited about nightlife on the boardwalk. But recently, she would eat her dinners with Madame in the kitchen -- who taught her how to cook. Ironically, it was more thrilling to spend time with the mysterious old woman and watch her slowly let down her walls as she reminisced to Fuchsia about her past.

"Uh..." Fuchsia scratched her head, "I think I'll go out tonight."

"Alright," Madame smiled and firmly nodded.

Fuchsia pulled out the cash from her purse -- or what used to be Madame's purse -- and remembered how Madame had suggested she get herself a haircut. Walking down the boardwalk, she stopped in front of a small shop called "CHIC CUTS" and headed inside.

"What kinda haircut you lookin' for?" The woman asked.

"I don't know, uh... regular?" Fuchsia shrugged.

"A lil' trim? Sure, sure, I got ya."

"Wait," Fuchsia suddenly stopped her.

"Uh-huh?"

"Can you make it pink?"

The hairdresser's eyes lit up, "oh, pink! Yes, hun, of course!"

"And chop it all off!" Fuchsia added, throwing her hands in the air. She was ready for change.

"'Kay!" She cheered.

Forty-five minutes later and Fuchsia stared at herself in the mirror -- pink hair, just a few inches below her ears.

"Oh, hun," the hairdresser gushed, "you look dazzling!"

"Dazzling?" Fuchsia put her hand on her heart. No one had called her that since back in her acting days. "Why, thank you."

After grabbing a personal pizza for herself, Fuchsia headed towards the beach to eat on the sand. The air was cool with a slight breeze. With her new hairstyle, nearly everyone was staring at her. It was fun, pretending she was a famous mermaid again.

With no one else in sight, Fuchsia sang...

"It's been so long, since you've been gone
My Captain, sailing across the sea.
Now here I am, a part of the plan
To save our species, and humanity.
We'll be together, goddess and god
Our love will be the world's cure.
So quit pretending that this is the ending
I know someday, you'll be back for more."

And just then, out of seemingly nowhere, lo and behold: the Captain appeared right in front of Fuchsia's face! He had his full uniform on -- even his cap!

Heart pounding like a drum Fuchsia screamed in astonishment, "Captain?!"

"'Tis I!" He confidently nodded, chest facing up towards the sky.

Fuchsia froze in absolute bewilderment.

"Your hair..." he took note of her new, pink bob, "It's fantastic!"

Fuchsia felt her face heat up in redness, "thanks," she sheepishly replied.

"Let's go!" He sharply threw his hands in the air.

"Huh?" she asked.

"Let's go on my ship!" He reiterated.

"Seriously?"

"What, what's wrong?" The self-assured expression on his face immediately fell into an expression of total despair.

"You know what happened last time..." Fuchsia cautiously reminded him.

"But this is now," he urged in excitement, "Fuchsia, I heard your poem you just sang, I heard your other poem from before, too!"

"You did? You heard all that?" Fuchsia covered her face.

"Stop now, don't be shy," he playfully teased.

Fuchsia still felt frozen. Seeing his face now, all she could think about was what Madame had prophesied for them -- their destiny as the new Mother Mermaid and Father Merman, goddess and god of the sea. She felt an invisible weight sinking upon her and nearly swallowing her whole. She felt her throat closing up. She couldn't move, barely couldn't even speak.

After a moment of silence, the Captain continued with, "I love you!"

"I love you too," Fuchsia said -- very flatly, completely passionless.

The Captain sighed in frustration, "*do you?*"

Fuchsia couldn't believe it -- she had been dying for the Captain to come and rescue her, ever since their failed boatride. Yet now that he was here, it was all too overwhelming. There was more vulnerability between the two of them now than ever before -- she knew *everything* -- the shapeshifting, the spying, and their enormous destiny that awaited them.

It was her dream come true, standing right there in front of her -- and yet she could not accept it. The nausea sunk in again, and this time she couldn't blame it on seasickness.

After a short silence, the Captain awkwardly asked, "...should I go?"

"No," Fuchsia forced herself to say -- but it didn't feel right.

"What's wrong, Fuch? Why are you being so distant?" He walked closer to her, attempting to pull her in with his arms.

In reflex, Fuchsia impulsively jumped backwards -- "I'm sorry! I didn't mean to do that!" She felt her whole body clench and tense up.

"I see," the Captain reluctantly nodded.

"No, no!" Fuchsia screamed, "I did *not* mean to jump back like that! It was a reflex! It wasn't intentional!" She stepped forward, reaching her arms back towards the Captain. But it was too late.

"Clearly, you're very hesitant. Look -- you're either all in or all out. Don't send me mixed messages."

"I'm *not!*" Fuchsia cried out, "I *do* want to be with you -- I don't know, it feels like something is holding me back, and it's out of my control. I want to be with you *so bad.*"

"You're scared, aren't you? Just pretend I'm Zale! Anyone! Do you want me to shapeshift into someone else? Would that help?"

"No, I want you to be yourself, I just..." she shifted uncomfortably.

"I knew you'd do this."

"Do what? Captain, no, take me with you right now!" She pleaded.

Without even saying goodbye, he disappeared.

"Oh, come on!" Fuchsia screamed out, as if he was still there, "just the *slightest* amount of resistance from me and you run! Can't you see, I'm trying? I'm trying to be brave, I'm really, really trying!"

XVIII. THE NEW MOTHER MERMAID

T oday, it was Fuchsia's birthday.

"I'm twenty," she flatly informed Madame upon waking up that morning.

"Happy birthday, young dear!" Madame cheered.

"It doesn't feel like my birthday at all," she observed.

"Why's that?"

"I really blew it with the Captain," Fuchsia confessed, "at this point, I think it's impossible for us to ever be together. It's going to seriously take a divine miracle."

"Don't lose hope," Madame assured.

That afternoon, washing dishes, Fuchsia randomly felt a strong burning in her heart. Turning off the sink, she scurried into the main room. And sure enough, the door burst open to a very familiar face -- no, three familiar faces! It was her sisters!

"Amber! Turquoise! Emerald!" Fuchsia called out their names in absolute shock. It was incredibly strange to see them with human legs.

"We found you!" They shouted with relief.

Madame looked over, "can I help you?"

"It's my three sisters!" Fuchsia explained in excitement, "the ones I've told you about!"

"Hello," Madame politely greeted.

"Hi," the three sisters greeted back.

"Fuchsia, we need to talk, *now*," Amber impatiently urged.

"Alright..." Fuchsia skeptically agreed. "Madame, may I step outside for a moment?"

"Sure," she nodded.

Fuchsia took her three sisters outside, around the back of the shop where they could get some privacy.

"Mother Mermaid!" Amber exclaimed, nearly out of breath, "she kidnapped us and has been holding us hostage!"

"Huh?" Fuchsia was absolutely perplexed, "Mother Mermaid? She held you against your will?" Something felt very *off*...

"Yes!" Turquoise urged, "she had the three of us locked up behind bars! Somehow, we finally managed to escape! We had to find you right away!"

"Why would she lock you girls up?" Fuchsia furrowed her eyebrows, "and how'd you get legs?"

"That's beside the point!" Amber exclaimed impatiently, "Mother Mermaid is evil, and we need your help!"

Covering her face in absolute confusion, Fuchsia replied, "but why -- why would she do this?"

"I told you, out of evilness!" Amber threw her hands up, "now, hurry, there's no time!"

"I don't want to go back to the sea!" Fuchsia refused, with her arms crossed, "this is where I belong. I'm working hard and I'm going to help a lot of people someday. I'm not just swimming in circles all day, partying and feasting! This life is difficult, but at least it's something *real.*"

"You don't understand," Turquoise shook her head, "you've got a mission down there in the ocean. We need your help. This is as real as it gets!"

"No, I *don't* understand!" Fuchsia fired back, "will someone please explain to me what is actually going on?"

Finally, Emerald spoke up, and explained, "Mother Mermaid needs you back in the ocean right now! She asked for our help -- at first, we refused -- but then she had us imprisoned and refused to set us free unless we found you!"

Turquoise added, "and we're still locked up. Mother Mermaid created carbon copies of us -- with legs -- as our only chance of freedom, to wrangle you in."

Amber joined, "we have a time limit. If we can't bring you back in the next few minutes, we'll perish. That's why I'm saying, you have to come with us, *now*! There's no time for stories!"

"I don't even have my tail anymore!" Fuchsia exclaimed.

Amber told her, "Mother Mermaid will give it back to you. C'mon, we have to go!"

Heavily sighing, Fuchsia felt completely cornered. Leaving Oceana Paradise was the last thing she wanted, but there was no way she would gamble with her sisters's lives. And so, she agreed to return to the sea.

Stepping back into the psychic hut, Fuchsia asked Madame, "can I please take a quick break? I promise to make it as fast as possible!"

Without words, Madame simply nodded.

To her surprise, Fuchsia added, "it might be a little while, but I'll try to come back as soon as I can, it's an emergency!"

"You may go, no questions asked. Family comes first," Madame stated, no hesitation.

"Thank you, thank you so much," Fuchsia vigorously nodded before scurrying away.

Joining hands, the four sisters ran into the ocean and their legs magically morphed into mermaid tails. Still hand in hand, they swam together, diving deep at full speed like a cannonball, until they reached total darkness.

A distant light appeared, coming closer and closer until Fuchsia could vividly see it -- her three sisters locked in a steel jail cell. Quickly turning to her left and right, the carbon copies of her sisters had disintegrated.

"Here, we have her!" Amber screamed loudly behind bars, "now, set us all free!" She demanded.

"Fuchsia, we're not leaving without you!" Turquoise assured.

Gulping, Fuchsia's heart sank. She couldn't believe it. It was true, her sisters had been kidnapped, and they needed her rescue. She kicked herself for doubting them, yet still, she was in deep shock.

Finally, Mother Mermaid herself came forward.

"Mother Mermaid?" She pleaded in fear, teary-eyed, "how *could* you?"

"It was my only option," Mother Mermaid replied with a powerful and echoey voice.

"B-but -- you're kind, you're benevolent... you'd never do such a thing," Fuchsia stuttered.

"Let me explain."

"Try me!" Fuchsia threw her hands in the air.

"I need your help."

"You're Mother Mermaid! You're all-powerful! You don't need anybody's help!"

"Even goddesses need help sometimes. Listen here, I did what I had to do. It was the only way to bring you back to me. I kept using magic to force you here, but your energy was far too resistant. I tried summoning the Captain here, to use him as bait, but likewise his energy kept opposing me. And so, I had no choice but to use your sisters as bait. There is an urgent matter I must discuss with you."

"Just do what she says, Fuchsia!" Turquoise urged, "don't bother fighting!"

"I told you, she's pure evil!" Amber cut in.

"Silence!" Mother Mermaid impatiently screamed, locking their lips up so they couldn't speak.

Horrified, Fuchsia shrieked in fright, "oh my gosh!"

"Now listen to me, Fuchsia, and respect your goddess," Mother Mermaid demanded.

"What do you want!?"

"I need you back here in the ocean. You have been divinely called into an important mission. You cannot continue living on land. Your time is up!"

"I like it there," she explained, "I like working and striving every day. I've already found my destiny. I'm going to become a psychic healer and cure the humans. And then the merpeople will unite, and we will all live happily in peace. The mermaids and mermen can teach the humans how to let go of greed and materialism, to relax and let go, and save the environment before they destroy themselves again. Meanwhile, the humans can show us the benefits of having goals, working hard, and we no longer have to hide from them in fear. We can unite in harmony!"

In response, "oh, Fuchsia, that sounds like a beautiful dream. But how can you look your goddess in the eyes and claim a different destiny? That is arrogance."

"You may be more powerful than me, more magical too, but that does not mean you know what's best for me. Only *I* know what's best for me."

"It's because I can see things that you can't."

"Yeah, like what?"

"I can see the future, and I can see what's deep in your heart."

Fuchsia paused before replying, instead, she could feel Mother Mermaid seeing right through her and reading her mind. It was an unsettling feeling. And even more unsettling, was that she knew the answer... it was the Captain... he was deep in her heart. So deep now, that it had become buried -- like a pearl, covered in the sand of hopes and dreams that distracted her.

What was so appealing about the land, the human world, was the immense distraction -- the mix of smells coming from the beach, the restaurants, the sunscreen and cheap cologne... the sounds of people talking over one another, the seagulls gawking, the street performers with their drums and guitars... and the endless sights of such diverse people wearing all different kinds of outfits, little animals running around, and so many houses and buildings painted all different colors. It was all such a pleasant distraction from the aching loneliness inside her soul.

The ocean was bare, quiet, and dark blue. There was so much peace here, that it was a disturbing peace. Every day in the sea was the same -- hunting, drinking, and partying. On the land, there was always something happening, and every day was different. There were always new customers with new dramas, coming to Madame for a reading.

Mother Mermaid continued, with a heavy sigh, "I'm about to die, which is why I need you to take my place. You will be the new Mother Mermaid and serve as guidance for your merpeople. You will be a healer, not for humankind, but for mermankind. They need you more than ever, more than the humans do."

"You're about to die?" Fuchsia's heart sank, "but, you're immortal, aren't you?"

"I'm afraid not," she explained, "I'm dying of a broken heart. I have ruled too long without my counterpart god, Father Merman."

"Who is Father Merman?"

"He was my other half. I tried to rule alone for as long as I could, knowing that no one else could replace him. And now my time has come, I could only stall for so long..."

"How did Father Merman die, then? Did you... break his heart?" Fuchsia hesitated.

"Look, time is limited. I am moments away from perishing! All I ask is that you let me die in peace by assuring you will take my place. Can you do that, for your fellow mermaids and mermen?" She gazed deep into Fuchsia's eyes.

"But, why me?" Fuchsia huffed.

"You are the chosen one -- the only mermaid who has what it takes."

"Surely there must be someone, anyone else who'd be a better fit! I'm not that smart, I make a lot of mistakes, and you said so yourself, that I'm arrogant! So, why? Why me!?"

"You are the only one with enough wisdom and magic."

Still unable to understand, Fuchsia felt cornered. She couldn't let Mother Mermaid die alone, she couldn't let her down like this. And so, she surrendered.

"Okay!" Fuchsia proclaimed, "I'll do it!"

Clasping her hands together in satisfaction, Mother Mermaid happily announced, "now let's find your Captain!"

"What do you mean?" Her heart pounded.

"As I said, this is no job to do alone. You'll perish too soon. So, you and the Captain shall rule together! I couldn't bring him here with my magic alone, but the two of us together, we can summon him effortlessly!"

"Really?" Fuchsia's eyes lit up, glimmering with hope, "you can help bring him back to me?"

"Yes!" Mother Mermaid ferociously nodded, "now, place your hands in mine."

Holding back, Fuchsia stopped herself, "wait."

"There's no time!"

"The Captain already told me he was king once, and that it ruined him. That's why he left the ocean in the first place. He doesn't want that power."

"But you two would be more than king and queen now, you would be Father and Mother -- inheriting all of my magic!"

"That's even worse!"

"Wake up, dear child! You have been crying over the Captain for more than two years now! This is the chance you've been waiting for!"

"No!" Fuchsia firmly refused, "I'll surrender my plans in order to fulfill yours, but I will not subject the Captain to that. He deserves to live his own life. And if he wanted to be with me, we wouldn't have to resort to magic like this. He'd already be here. This feels like manipulation. If he wants me, he can find me! I'm not forcing him towards me like this!"

With yet another heavy sigh, Mother Mermaid told her, "I cannot fight with you any longer. We have wasted enough time. I'm already beginning to vanish. If you want to rule alone, so be it. But promise me that you'll provide the merpeople with the spiritual guidance they need. Do not abandon them, or there will be chaos."

"I can't," Fuchsia shook her head, "I can't force him to be here. He has already told me before that he is not interested in this power, that he has been king before, that he knows it brings corruption. And I'm sorry to say Mother Mermaid, you have proved to me that you are also corrupted with power — bribing me, kidnapping me, locking up my sisters, using magic for evil."

Mother Mermaid placed her hands on Fuchsia and explained, "in just a few seconds, I am going to perish. My power will be transferred to you. The next man you kiss on the lips will share this power. I highly suggest you share your power, because love grants immortality, otherwise you will be forced to find a new mermaid to take over before you perish. Now, in this final moment that I am still alive, are you sure you do not want to use our combined power to bring the Captain back to you?"

"I'm sure!" Fuchsia nodded.

"Be the new Mother Mermaid — not for me, but for the survival of our entire species!" were Mother Mermaid's final words, as her body disintegrated into dust and swirled around Fuchsia's body a few times before absorbing into her skin.

Completely moved, tears were running down Fuchsia's face. The next thing she knew, she was once again standing on top of a large boulder standing before her merpeople.

She immediately spotted her sisters. They swam towards her.

"Oh, thank goodness," Fuchsia placed her hand on her heart in relief, "you're free!"

"What happened to Mother Mermaid?" Amber asked.

"She..." Fuchsia paused, because she was still in shock over what had happened, "she's gone!"

"What do you mean 'gone'?" Turquoise asked.

"She's... she's dead."

Amber, Turquoise, and Emerald gasped.

Fuchsia continued, "she died and passed all her magic to me. Apparently I'm the only one who was fit to take her place, but I didn't want to do it. I just wanted to save you girls."

Amber inquired, "she passed all her magic to you?"

Fuchsia innocently shrugged, "yeah, whatever that means!" And then added, "but I don't want to take her place! I wanna go back to Oceana Paradise and live with the humans!"

"Then go back," Amber assured.

"Seriously?" Turquoise said to Amber, "you don't think she should stay?"

With a sigh, Amber concluded, "Fuchsia has always been different -- unlike us. Mermaids are supposed to spend their whole lives under the sea, but Fuchsia has never been an ordinary mermaid. So let her do what makes her happy."

"Wow," Fuchsia beamed, "thank you, Amber. I'm beyond grateful that you understand."

"Promise you'll visit us," Emerald added.

"Of course," Fuchsia smiled.

"But what about Mother Mermaid?" Turquoise asked, "if you don't fulfill her spot, what's going to happen?"

"What did Mother Mermaid do anyway?" Amber questioned, "she just sat in her cave all day in isolation. People would pray to her, but it's not like she ever did much back."

"Yeah," Turquoise agreed, "I don't even know if she was ever that important."

"So you three can take her place?" Fuchsia hoped.

"Sure," Amber shrugged, "I'm just happy that evil thing is gone now. I can't believe she kidnapped us like that!"

The four sisters turned to the crowd, and Turquoise said, "I think they're waiting for you to make a speech."

Fuchsia had been so focused on her sisters, that she failed to notice the pack of mermaids and mermen staring at her in awe, hypnotized, anticipating her speech. It was deja vu. But this time, Fuchsia wouldn't have it.

So, she announced in her loudest voice, "mermaids and mermen, I'm here to tell you that Mother Mermaid is no longer with us."

Gasps and small chatter arose.

"I'm here to take her place. And my first order as Mother Mermaid, is to see you all free. I don't belong here -- I have to go. But I trust that you can all survive on your own."

Going on, Fuchsia turned to her sisters, "my three sisters -- Amber, Turquoise, and Emerald -- they're here if needed be. But I trust that you all can survive just fine without her."

Hugging her sisters goodbye, Fuchsia transported back to her true home — beach town Oceana Paradise. It had only been less than a day she was gone, yet the heaviness of it made it seem like so much longer. As she tucked herself into bed, the stray cat returned, jumping into her arms and purring loudly.

XIV. A TASTE
OF DEATH

By the time Fuchsia returned home, to the psychic shop, in the little beach town of Oceana Paradise, it was already past dark. She lost track of the time she was gone, it couldn't have been longer than an hour or so, and yet it felt like it had been days. So she tucked herself straight into bed, emotionally exhausted.

The next morning, Fuchsia scurried downstairs to great Madame.

"How long was I gone?" She pondered.

"You were out all night!" Madame explained.

Furrowing her eyebrows, attempting to make sense of it all, Fuchsia insisted, "are you sure?"

"Why -- did it feel longer or shorter than that?"

"Well..." she thought hard, "both, actually."

Raising one eyebrow, Madame commanded with skepticism, "dear child, tell me what happened."

With a deep inhale, Fuchsia went on to explain everything. She went into great depth about everything -- how Mother Mermaid kidnapped her sisters and used them as bait to bring her back to the ocean, how she refused to use magic to summon the Captain, how Mother Mermaid died right in front of her and transferred her powers, insisting she take her place, and lastly, after assuring the safety of her sisters, how she fled the scene and returned back to her true home.

Exasperated, Fuchsia took a deep exhale, and concluded with, "so, that's about it!"

Madame gazed at her blankly, trying to take it all in.

"You don't believe me," Fuchsia rolled her eyes.

Without a word, Madame gently grabbed Fuchsia's hand and guided her to the royal chair where she conducts her readings. And then, she ripped off the sheet that covers her magic crystal ball.

"Are you serious?" Fuchsia's jaw dropped, "the crystal ball? You're going to give me another reading?"

"No," Madame shook her head, "I want you to read."

Her heart dropped, as she replied, "I may regret asking... but why?"

Madame paused for a moment.

"I know, I know, I ask too many questions!" Fuchsia backtracked with regret, "forget it!"

"I'll tell you why," Madame answered, "your story. The way you had an opportunity to abuse your power, and you didn't."

Fuchsia tilted her head with curiosity, hoping Madame could tell her more.

"You could have summoned the Captain with enough magic between you and Mother Mermaid, and you resisted. Good."

"Well, yeah," Fuchsia explained, "I really, really, really wanted to see him again. But he already told me that he didn't want that kind of power, that he had that chance before, and it almost ruined him."

Madame nodded.

"I don't know if I want to see... actually," Fuchsia said with caution.

"You don't?"

"What if I don't see... the future you showed me when I first came here... what if I ruined it?"

Madame placed her hand on Fuchsia's shoulder and said, "destiny is destiny."

So Fuchsia took a deep breath, braced herself and began to gaze into the crystal ball, focusing hard on her intuition.

Instead of seeing her future, Fuchsia saw her past. She saw herself as a wee toddler, learning how to swim. And her parents were there.

"No, no," Fuchsia shook her head. But she couldn't look away.

Tears streamed down her face as she saw them speak to her with such sweetness. Her father placed a toy crown on her head and said, "you will be queen someday!"

"Stop!" Fuchsia shouted, but the vision only became more vivid. Her mother placed a kiss on her cheek and held her in her arms.

Fuchsia continued to watch as her baby self twirled in circles, trying to keep balance. Quite a wobbly, graceless child she was!

Her parents giggled at their little daughter with amusement. And their laughter was so pure.

A group of young and mischievous boys came by and started

throwing pebbles at baby Fuchsia. But her parents stopped them, furious at their behavior. Her mother held baby Fuchsia tightly in her arms, fiercely clenching her tight. Her father screamed at the little boys with fury.

"These aren't my parents. They're being so protective. My parents were nasty and awful," Fuchsia mumbled to herself.

A crying baby Fuchsia licked a sea popsicle as her parents continued to comfort her.

"ENOUGH!" Fuchsia burst out, throwing the crystal ball across the room and smashing it into a billion pieces, shards of glass flying about.

And then, Fuchsia shut her eyes and fell into a very deep sleep.

A few moments later she woke up, unsure of how much time had passed. There was total darkness.

"Is this a dream or real life?" she thought out loud. The only time she ever had this feeling was during a lucid dream, or that one time she accidentally nibbled on too much seaweed.

Suddenly a blurry figure appeared. Fuchsia blinked a few times, but couldn't see straight.

"You ruined your destiny!" said the voice.

"What?" Fuchsia cried out.

And then it became more clear — it was Mother Mermaid.

"Your destiny!" Mother Mermaid continued, "It was your final chance!"

"For what?"

"To be with the Captain! It was your only chance to bring him back!"

"But I couldn't, I–"

"Yes, you could! Why didn't you fight for him? Fight for your merpeople?"

"I didn't, I–"

"You abandoned them all! Not only did you disappoint the Captain, you disappointed your people! You were supposed to be their spiritual leader! Now, they've all gone mad! They're all drunk off their arses, rioting and destroying one another, completely lost!"

"They... they are?"

"YES!"

"But I've only been gone for one night!" She pleaded.

"No," Mother Mermaid disagreed, "it's been one year now."

"No it hasn't," Fuchsia furiously shook her head, "I left the ocean, went back to the psychic and fell asleep, woke up the next morning, and that was all! It's been one night!"

"No," Mother Mermaid continued disagreeing, and explained, "you went back to work, you gradually learned to become a psychic, and now it has been exactly one year later. You're twenty-one years old. And your sea village has destroyed themselves, the same way humans are on an endless path of destruction."

"What!?" Fuchsia exclaimed in terror, "it's been a whole year? What happened to my memory?"

"You're in a deep trance."

"How is any of this my fault?"

"Because you are the *NEW MOTHER MERMAID*, whether you accept it or not! And you chose *not* to accept it! Without your presence there, they lost their spirituality and have gone mad! All you had to do was be there for them! Summon your captain! And fulfill your destiny!"

"I can go back!" she pleaded.

"*NO!*" she shouted, "There's *NO TURNING BACK!*"

"Bring me back to sea, I'll be their leader, I don't care. I'll quit my job, I'll leave Madame. I'll even summon the Captain against his will. I don't want madness upon the merpeople and I certainly don't want to be the reason why! I'm just a mermaid! I just wanted to live a normal mermaid life like everyone else! I did not ask for this power! But I'll do what you say if it's truly my destiny!"

"It's too late," she said in a quieter, mundane voice, now practically emotionless, "They're too far gone, you can't help them at this point. And forget about the Captain. It was already too late before, but I gave you one final chance out of pity to bring him back, and you denied it.

Fuchsia ground her teeth in vexation and defended herself, "he didn't want to, and I was not going to force him against his will, that is *not* love!"

"You fight for him!"

"If it was meant to be then I wouldn't have to use magic to have him! That would be an abuse of power!"

"Who decides if it's meant to be? *You* decide if it's meant to be."

"No, no, please, stop it!" Fuchsia covered her face and started shaking, "we will be together, we will! It's destiny!"

"It's destiny's greatest enemy — free will. I want you to know that you have lost your chance. There's no recovery from this. Better luck next lifetime," and just like that, poof, she was gone. And it was back to total darkness.

Fuchsia stood there, alone and scared in the dark. "Hello!?" she called out, but there was no one there. "Mother Mermaid, come back!" she pleaded, face completely flushed. "Please!" she cried, "I'm sorry!" She waited, and still nothingness... "What happened to forgiveness?"

Fuchsia felt a gravitational pull through her body as if she was beginning to fly, and then looked down to see herself at the psychic, sitting in front of the crystal ball. It was an out-of-body experience. Except it looked like she hadn't actually thrown the crystal ball across the room. Instead, her head was face down on the table as if she had slammed her head straight into the crystal ball. There was a pool of blood dripping from the crack in her forehead.

"If only you had told me Mother Mermaid transferred her power to you! You wouldn't have had a vision this strong!" A completely broken and distraught Madame weeped as an ambulance came rushing in.

"Did... I die...?" Fuchsia thought out loud in utter shock.

Her vision once again became fuzzy as darkness took back over. Nothing but darkness. But the feeling was warmer this time.

"Honey," an oddly familiar voice called out.

Fuchsia turned around and was astounded to see her mother and father standing right there! She could see part of their faces, but not their full bodies. Reaching out, she attempted to give them a hug, yet couldn't.

"Please, do not yet come to the other side, not yet," they begged.

"I feel that I must," Fuchsia said, teary-eyed, "I found the one thing worth living for, and I lost it. So I'm leaving this life and hoping I'll find him in the next."

"Don't give up," her mother said, and her voice really made Fuchsia's heart glow, and she felt like her three-year old self again. And the memory came back to her. It was a Sunday evening. Her parents were teaching her how to swim, but a rush of hungry children came swarming, completely throwing Fuchsia off balance. Her mother offered to take a break, but Fuchsia just kept saying, "no!" She was so determined to learn to swim, she wouldn't let anything distract her. But then a group of little boys came by throwing pebbles at her, and that's when she burst into tears. Her mother comforted her, and she felt so safe in her arms. The boys' parents were so embarrassed that they demanded they apologize and hand over their entire collection of rare pebbles. And Fuchsia, Mom, and Dad, all played with the pebbles together. It was a joyous memory she kept suppressed her whole life. Now it felt clear as day.

With joy in her heart, Fuchsia remembered that determination she had as a child to learn to swim, just as she still has today to keep going. She fought as hard as she could with her mind, peacefully parting ways with her parents, now only seeing blotches of darkness, and then finally a clear picture of herself again. She was in the hospital.

"C'mon, c'mon," Fuchsia thought, looking down upon herself, "stay alive!"

A wave of exhaustion hit sharply throughout her body. But she just kept fighting, harder and harder. She could no longer *think* of any distinct words, she could only *feel* at this point. Another wave of exhaustion.

She was standing still, but felt as if she had just run a marathon. She kept pushing against this feeling, kept reminding herself of all the reasons to smile, kept picturing that image of herself with her parents as a child. Another, much harder, wave of exhaustion pulsated throughout her body as blotches of darkness started appearing in her vision and everything was getting fuzzier again.

Fuchsia fought with all of her might to remember that scene, playing and laughing with her parents, a time when happiness was greatest in her heart. Her vision became clear again, and then immediately became twice as blurry as more darkness took over. Another wave of exhaustion so painful she had no choice but to let go of resistance. Darkness everywhere.

"I should have fought harder..." was the final phrase to run through her head.

There she was again, in total darkness. Yet this time, there was no voice or figure coming out. She couldn't speak. She couldn't hear her own thoughts. She couldn't think.

All was darkness.

And darkness was all.

Until a ray of light appeared.

The light grew stronger and brighter.

It was coming towards her.

Closer and closer.

Until she was completely blinded.

And just as Fuchsia felt her soul getting unstoppably sucked into a vacuum, she could feel the Captain's energy, with such force, velocity, and intensity. Suddenly, Fuchsia felt his energy moving towards the light, as her soul moved away from it. Now she was back in darkness.

It wasn't until the light had completely disappeared, when Fuchsia could begin to comprehend what had just happened. It was him -- it was the Captain -- or was it? Her thoughts were coming back now. She could think again!

Opening her eyes, she was back in the sea, surrounded by dark blue. She was back in her normal body. She could feel her heartbeat and her blood flowing through her veins. She could feel her breath moving in and out of her lungs as her stomach expanded and contracted. She could feel the heat flushed upon her cheeks. She could feel. She could think. She... was... alive.

"What is going on?" Fuchsia barely managed to whisper, struggling to get her voice back.

"Fuchsia, you didn't listen to me," Mother Mermaid's voice announced from nowhere.

"Mother Mermaid!?" Fuchsia looked around with puzzlement, "where are you? Are you alive?"

She continued, "I am still dead, but you can hear me still because you just came back from the other side. You are still half-dead, slowly coming back to life."

"What happened?"

"It's been a year since I died and transferred the rest of my magic to you."

"That's not possible," Fuchsia denied, her voice a bit stronger now, "it couldn't have been longer than a day."

"Your magic spun out of control. You didn't isolate yourself in safety like I told you to. You went straight back to the land, to that beach town, and continued working as if nothing happened. Each day, countless people walking by, countless customers coming in and out, you faced many psychic attacks. Your magic spiraled, it messed with your memory, that's why you can't remember anything. It just kept on suppressing itself, until finally it all erupted like a volcano. And then... you died."

Choking up, Fuchsia replied, "is that truly so? But I'm alive now, aren't I? Or am I still dreaming?"

"There's no dreams, it's all real. And yes, you've come back to life. Do you know how?"

"No," she gulped.

"The Captain, he came to your rescue."

"He... he did?"

"Yes, he did."

"But how?"

"You two are destined soulmates, therefore you share the same energy. So when I transferred my magic to you, it was also transferred to him, and he experienced an unknown surge. And then when your magic spun out of control, simultaneously, so did his! And as you were pulled to the other side, so was he! Except, the difference was that he had a little more strength inside of him -- for he has been spending his time completely alone, on his ship. He hasn't been boggled down by so many different energies like you have. With the last tiny ounce of his energy, he could have used it to save himself, pull himself away from the light, and come back to life."

"But... he didn't..."

"Instead of saving himself, he used the last of his energy to save *you.*"

"He rescued me? And he's gone now, because of me? Wha-what happened this past year? What have I been doing, nothing but work? Did the Captain ever find me?"

"Oh," Mother Mermaid nearly chuckled, "it took a divine intervention for you two to finally find each other. Over the last year, you've been working hard -- you became an impressive psychic, Madame taught you well. You've been giving wonderful readings. But you have not been protecting yourself."

"What has the Captain been doing this whole time!?"

"He has visited you often, almost every day, very briefly, in other forms -- curious cats and passerby humans. But no, you two have been stubbornly avoiding each other, to come face-to-face. Like I said, it took a true divine intervention."

"Why did he save me if we were still in separation?"

"It took his final moment of death to realize what was right. It is not until one's ego is shed, when it is fully understood that loving someone means putting that person first -- battling against one's pride and fighting for that person."

"Surely, there must be a way I can bring him back! I can fight for him!"

"I'm afraid it's too late."

"No, it can't be! Tell me our love is strong enough! Please! Tell me a miracle is possible!"

"I can use the last of my dying energy to bring you his holograph. That way you can say your peace."

"His holograph? What does that mean? And don't go back to the other side, Mother Mermaid! Don't do it because of me!"

"Oh, sweetie, I am on my way back there, no matter the case. It has been my time for long enough. I am grateful to be so touched by the Captain's love for you, that I was able to come back to life for these mere few minutes. Now, I must be going."

"Wait!" Fuchsia cried out, "I have so many more questions! I'm still so confused! Please bring back the Captain, please!"

As Fuchsia screamed her words, Mother Mermaid inevitably disappeared into the abyss. And then, immediately, the Captain appeared. Although, Fuchsia was not even sure if it was him anymore, if it was just a "holograph" or another illusion. At this point, Fuchsia had completely lost her concept of reality. There was no distinguishing between real and imagined.

For all she knew, she could open her eyes at any moment -- and this whole thing would've been a dream. That was what she hoped for, at least. All this confusion was unbearable. She simply wanted to wake up back to age eighteen, the morning she ventured to the surface of the sea, and met her dear Captain. No fights, no distance, no complications -- just a fresh start, and a happily ever after.

XX. END OF THE RAINBOW

Now, Fuchsia stood face-to-face with an image of the Captain, unsure if it was merely a projection, or hallucination -- or if it was genuinely him.

"Captain!" she couldn't help but exclaim, flooded with joy to see him again, rushing towards him in a frenzy.

"Wait," he stopped her, holding up his hands, causing a wave of water to push Fuchsia backwards, so she couldn't reach him. The Captain continued, "I am only a hologram, I cannot be touched."

"Is it you? Are you really there? Can you hear me?"

"Who's to say if the Captain is long gone, or not..."

Rolling her eyes and shaking her head exasperation, Fuchsia replied, "you're not real. You're just here for me to say my peace, to break free from my conscience. You're just a dream, aren't you?"

The Captain was silent.

So, Fuchsia went on, skeptically raising an eyebrow, "but I know it was really you, all those other times. You were Zale, the lifeguard boy. You were Rainbow, the beautiful girl. You were the stray, black cat, who meowed at my window during the full moons. So, tell me, who are you?"

The Captain remained silent, yet slightly moved his lips as if there was something waiting to come out, but it wouldn't.

And then Fuchsia continued, her voice gaining passion, "I know who you are -- I'll tell you!"

The Captain tried to keep a poker face, however, became a bit scared and defensive, like he was about to be told off, attacked by the gorgeous mermaid's sharp tongue. He tightened his muscles and braced himself for the worst.

Instead, Fuchsia's voice softened with her eyes growing wide, as she spoke, "you are... the love of my life," she glowed.

With a sigh, and a bow of the head, the Captain at last, replied, "no, I'm not... and I'm no captain, hardly even a sailor... just a cowardly merman who ran away from the world."

In strong opposition, Fuchsia defended, "what are you talking abou--"

The Captain stopped her, "--I'm not this starstruck image you have of me in your head. I'm not this brave man exploring the seven seas -- I'm living my life on the run, so that no one tracks my tail. I am not 'the Captain.'"

"And I'm not a mermaid!" Fuchsia assured, before shortly pausing, "I mean, yes, I'm literally a mermaid. But, but, I'm not that actress I played on the stage for everyone, I'm not the superstar I acted like I was before I met you."

"I know," he agreed, "you gave up that celebrity life so you could disguise yourself as a janitor, working hard and aspiring to learn from Madame."

"Yes, I did. I did it all for you."

"You wanted to heal the humans and unite them with the mer-people, so you could be everyone's hero."

"I wanted to heal myself and unite us," Fuchsia came slightly closer, yet not so close that she would get pushed away again, "I only wanted to be *your* hero."

The Captain slightly furrowed his eyebrows.

"Everything else was my distraction," she added.

The Captain let himself get only a bit closer, while still keeping a fair amount of distance between her and himself. And then he muttered softly, "are you still distracted?"

Fuchsia remained put, keeping space between the two, and replied, "I can't stop wondering, what happened, that day on the boat? We were about to have our happily ever after, and yet you threw it all away. What did I do?"

He sighed, and told her, "you didn't do anything. I became too inside my head and started overthinking everything. I was flooded with fear, and I let it get the best of me, instead of trusting you."

"How do I know that won't happen again?"

"You tell me first -- what happened on the day we first met? You had me in the palm of your hands and yet you pulled away. Why?"

"Well, I was also too deep inside my head. I couldn't trust you, I was absolutely terrified."

"And how do I know that won't happen again?"

"Haven't we been through quite the journey since we first met?"

"Likewise, since we sailed on my ship."

Fuchsia paused for a moment, and then said, "when I was a moment away from death, and I felt your energy, I *knew* -- I just knew. I couldn't see you with my eyes, couldn't hear you with ears, couldn't even remember who you were -- my thoughts and memories were gone! And yet, I *knew*! I knew it was you, I knew it was my one, true soulmate."

Now the Captain paused as well, before stating, "that's exactly how I felt -- the moment we met. I was sailing towards you before I even saw you, before I even heard your captivating voice, singing in the distance. I wasn't traveling anywhere in particular, I simply let my soul take the wheel and lead me to my destiny. And there you were."

"And that's how I found you. I wasn't swimming anywhere specific, just following my heart."

"I wasn't hunting for mermaids."

"And I wasn't seeking out sailors."

"It just happened."

"It was..."

And together, they both exclaimed, "destiny!"

Without hesitation, the two reached in for a magical kiss on the lips. Eyes closed, arms wrapped around each other, and mouths pressed together. They felt a rush at the same time, followed by a swirl of glittering stars dancing around their bodies.

It was their fairytale. It was their happy ending. It was their happily ever after. And all was right in the world.

After their kiss, Fuchsia pulled the Captain back in, even closer now -- "don't ever leave," she commanded, yearning to prove her passion for him.

"Who are you giving orders to?" He teased, "I am your Captain."

"Oh!" She blushed, face turning red.

"I'm kidding," he gently squeezed her arms, "you're my goddess."

"You're my god," she gazed deep into his eyes.

"Come with me," he told her, and she nodded and followed without hesitation.

The Captain and the Mermaid teleported to the little beach town of Oceana Paradise. Their human legs were back. Fuchsia still had her short, pink hair. They stood on a small, private dock that faced the crashing waves of the shore. Facing one another, the Captain held Fuchsia's hands together, pressing against her stomach.

He began, "when I came up with the name 'Zale,' I was passing by a beautiful diamond shop... and all I could think about was marrying you..."

Fuchsia silently nodded, letting him speak, curious as to what he was about to reveal.

"But those diamonds... they didn't seem to fit... I just couldn't picture you wearing one..."

"Oh?" Fuchsia skeptically nodded, wondering if she was about to be rejected, after everything they had just been through...

"So I found this," he swiftly leaned down on one knee and pulled out a ring with a rainbow pearl.

"Oh, goodness!" Fuchsia gasped -- it was the most colorful pearl she had ever seen, "I thought those things were white!"

"Ah, yes they are -- usually. But you are *not* usual, Fuchsia. I searched the entire sea for this precious pearl."

"I can't believe it!" She couldn't stop smiling.

"Will you..." the Captain began.

"Wait!" Fuchsia stopped him, watching the delightful smile on his face melt into horror. It was like their first encounter all over again. But Fuchsia wasn't going to reject him, she only had one simple question, before she could let him propose... "What is your name?"

"My name?" the Captain raised his eyebrows.

"Yeah," Fuchsia chuckled, "I've been calling you 'Captain' this whole time, surely that mustn't be your true birth name. For, you were born a merman, weren't you? What, ever, was your name back then?"

"I see," he nodded with slight disappointment, "I'm afraid my true name will break your perfect illusion of me."

"Silly, I already told you, there's no illusions left -- we have experienced death together -- all of these illusions have been shed, already!"

"Alright, if you must know..." he got off his knee and stood back up again. Looking away for a moment, he finally answered, "it's 'Cole.'"

"Oh!" Fuchsia nodded.

"I know, it's not what you were expecting -- it's not a title, it's not fancy, not even related to the ocean!"

"I like it," she smiled.

"Well, I don't," he furrowed his eyebrows, "it reminds me of the past, of a person I am no longer."

"Well, then, what shall I call you?"

The Captain remained silent, as Fuchsia pondered.

"I'll call you 'C'!" she exclaimed.

"C?" The Captain said.

"Yeah, 'C.' Like, as in, the 'sea.'"

"I like it," he smiled back.

"And, I'll still call you 'Captain' from time to time, because you'll always be my Captain," she blushed.

He tilted his head, sheepishly, as his face turned a little red.

"Oops, I'm sorry!" Fuchsia became flustered, "I ruined the moment, didn't I?"

"No, no," he assured, somewhat awkwardly, clearing his throat.

"Okay, go on!" she grinned, flashing her teeth.

And so, the Captain got back down on his knee, presenting the rainbow pearl ring, and announced, "Fuchsia, the absolute love of my life, will you marry me, and promise to spend eternity together?"

"Yes!" Fuchsia squealed, and as the Captain got up, she jumped into his arms with passion and exhilteration. She couldn't quite help but add, "when!?"

"Right now!" he immediately responded.

"Huh?" Fuchsia raised her eyebrows.

"There's no time like the present," he winked, still holding her in his arms.

"Are you serious?" Fuchsia looked around skeptically, wondering if she was in some type of dreamland.

"Well," he shrugged, "when do you think? Is there something you're waiting for?"

"No," Fuchsia shook her head with a slight pout on her face, looking nervous, "I just… there's just someone I want to say 'goodbye' to first."

"And who is that?" The Captain nearly froze. He wondered, was it another merman? Someone she wanted to give one final kiss to, before committing herself to him for life?

"Madame," she replied, as he sighed with relief. Fuchsia went on, "I feel like I left her hanging. I can't simply disappear. I owe her a proper farewell."

"Oh, of course!" the Captain enthused, "let's go see her, right now!"

"Perfect!" Fuchsia smiled.

"Unless you'd rather do that alone," he offered.

"No, no!" she furiously shook her head, "she has to meet you and see who you are!"

"Alright then!" he agreed.

And so, the Captain and the Mermaid walked into town, down the boardwalk, until they arrived at the front door of the little psychic shop. The "open" sign was glowing, and Fuchsia's heart fluttered with nervousness. She was worried about saying good-bye to Madame, who had served as not only a boss, but a mother figure to her.

"Madame!" Fuchsia announced with cheer, bursting inside with the Captain.

Catching her breath, Madame greeted, "there she is..."

Suddenly, Fuchsia's memory came back. She now recalled the past year, working closely with Madame, finally learning how to conduct readings. She gulped, also painfully remembering her collapse after the explosion of her pent-up magic. Madame had watched her body float to the ceiling before disintegrating, as she recited a prayer to safely guide her to the afterlife.

"Here we are," Fuchsia breathed out heavily, quite overwhelmed.

"Nice to meet you, Madame," the Captain nodded.

"I believe we have met before," Madame knowingly grinned, "Zale, was it?"

"She knows everything," Fuchsia rolled her eyes, "you knew this moment would happen, didn't you?" She giggled.

"Perhaps," Madame shrugged, "I knew it was... likely."

"It was *destined*," the Captain grasped Fuchsia's hand tighter now.

"So...?" Madame was patiently waiting for Fuchsia to say what she needed to say.

The Captain stepped back, letting Fuchsia and Madame have their moment.

So Fuchsia explained, "the Captain and I are taking responsibility as the new Father Merman and Mother Mermaid. That means we will have to live a life of seclusion, deep down in the bottom of the ocean. Obviously, we can still visit. I still plan to keep in touch with my sisters whenever I can. And I'd still like to come see you, if you'd like..."

"It was a pleasure being your boss," Madame warmly smiled, "usually the policy for leaving a job is giving two weeks notice. But for you, I'll make an exception. Go live your new life," she proudly assured.

"Oh, you've been more than a boss," Fuchsia urged, "although I've never had a boss before, you have been a teacher, a guru, a mother!"

"You are the closest thing I've had to a daughter -- besides my business of course, she's my baby," Madame laughed.

Fuchsia felt herself beginning to cry, as she went on, "I am so grateful for this journey you guided me through. I thought I wanted to be a psychic fortune teller, but I learned that what I truly want to be, is a psychic *healer*. Rather than telling people their future, I'd like to change their futures by healing their present."

"That's wonderful," Madame agreed.

"Plus," she added, "I could never be as accurate of a fortune teller as you."

"Honey, we all have our gifts. You shall be an excellent healer. I can see it... literally."

"The Captain and I will heal our merpeople. And hopefully, from time to time, when I visit here, I can work on healing some of the humans, too."

"That'd be lovely -- we can work together. Now, before you leave, I insist you let me conduct a formal reading on you two."

"Goodness, that would be a pleasure!" Fuchsia squealed, "c'mon, honey," she tugged her Captain over as the two of them sat down on the bench, facing Madame, who sat on her throne.

Madame pulled out the crystal ball and looked deep within.

"Aha," she nodded, "I am still seeing ten children... *at least!*"

The Captain looked at Fuchsia and raised an eyebrow.

Madame went on, "I'm seeing a very calm and peaceful life for you two..."

Fuchsia happily sighed with relief.

"For now," she added.

Fuchsia gulped.

"It's okay, honey," the Captain rubbed her back, before asking Madame, "what's going to happen?"

"There will be some challenges," Madame explained, "there will be ups and downs. It's not going to be perfect. You'll suffer many roadblocks and difficulties."

Fuchsia and the Captain nuzzled closer together.

And then Madame added, "but you are surely strong enough to get through it. These hardships will only make you stronger."

Fuchsia sighed with relief, as the Captain assured her, "you know we'll be fine, we're soulmates," he warmly smiled.

"No," Madame sharply shook her head, "I should mention that you two are not soulmates."

"What!?" Fuchsia bursted out, "Madame, that can't be possible!"

"You are *beyond* soulmates -- you are twin flames!"

"Ah," the Captain nodded with smugness, "I thought so."

"And what exactly *is* a twin flame?" Fuchsia questioned.

Madame explained, "when one soul splits into two bodies. It's the most challenging relationship to navigate, and requires the highest evolution of the soul in order to manifest. Soulmates are easy, they're walks in the park. Twin flames are the real deal, though, which explains why it took such a journey for you two to be together. And still, the journey is not over, it has only just begun."

"That's incredible," Fuchsia gushed, wide-eyed.

The Captain gazed at his mermaid with pure admiration.

"Very well," Madame nodded, "now, go and enjoy your new life together."

"Wait," Fuchsia stopped her, "can you tell us anything more specific? What exactly are these 'challenges' we'll eventually face, and how are we supposed to get through them?"

Madame hesitated for a second, and then replied, "I don't want to stir anything up, but... be sure to leave the past in the past. And always remember how much you love each other."

"What *about* the past?" Fuchsia questioned with agitation.

"My dear," Madame said calmly, "please, do not worry."

"No," Fuchsia demanded sternly, "I've seen you do about a million readings, Madame. I know you see very specific things and you never hold back. So please, what is it?"

"Fuchsia," the Captain cut in, "you know I have lived a long life, far long before you."

"Yeah..." Fuchsia suspiciously nodded, slowly.

"I told you the story of how long ago, I was a merman, too -- how I was their king for some time, before I ran away to live as Captain sailing the seas."

"Sure," she continued to nod, "I know."

"And you know how..."

"Oh, honey!" Madame impatiently rolled her eyes, "spit it out, already! I've got other customers waiting!"

"What!?" Fuchsia threw her hands in the air.

Finally, he told her, "there's been other mermaids before you -- although, none nearly as dazzling as you are, my dear."

"Okay..." Fuchsia responded with confusion, "I told you, I've kissed many, many other mermen besides you... I know you've had other mermaids in your life, even after you knew me. But we're moving forward now."

"Uh -- long, long before you, there were other connections... a few other connections... that lead to children."

Fuchsia felt her heart sink, unsure if she was hearing right, "you have kids?"

"Yes," he quickly nodded, "all grown up now, though…"

"Do you still see them?"

"Of course."

Fuchsia froze for a moment, and then asked, "why did you wait until *now* to tell me?"

"I mean, you didn't even know what my real name was up until a couple of minutes ago," he defended himself.

Madame jumped in, standing up, "okay, there's *lots* of things you two don't know about each other. But these are worldly things, they don't matter. What matters is that you two love each other, that you two are twin flames, destined to be together. Remember experiencing death with one another? Remember all that?"

"I guess," Fuchsia crossed her arms and furrowed her eyebrows.

"Oh, c'mon now, Fush, what did you expect?" he furrowed his eyebrows right back.

"Just honesty, is all!" she barked.

Lighting up a sage wand and waving it around the couple, Madame said, "you two have my deepest blessings."

Fuchsia watched the smoke fly around her, almost as if it was dancing in the air. And it made her giggle. And when the Captain heard her giggle, he couldn't help but giggle too.

"Goodbye, Madame," she sighed heavily, reaching her arms around for a big, bear hug.

"Goodbye, my starseed."

The next thing she knew, tears were running down Fuchsia's face.

"It's only temporary," the Captain told her with concern, "you can still visit any time."

"I know," Fuchsia sniffled, "it's just... *a lot...*" ending their hug, Fuchsia took a step back and continued, "it's been such a journey. I was a different person when I first walked through these doors. And now, here I am."

"I'll see you soon," Madame sympathized, before adding, "but I really do have a line of customers forming outside."

Fuchsia turned around to look out the front window and spotted a group of people waiting to come inside -- "oh!" she jumped, "let's go, Captain!"

"Come back soon," Madame smiled.

"We will," Fuchsia winked.

XXI. ...AND THEY LIVED HAPPILY EVER AFTER

T he couple ventured back down the boardwalk, this time on the sand, close to the crashing waves. It was much darker now, as dusk was shortly upon them. Holding hands, they both faced one another, gazing eye to eye.

"Do you still want to marry me?" the Captain asked in a low voice.

"Yes, of course!" Fuchsia squeezed him tight, "nothing could ever change that!"

"Do you think we're rushing into this?"

"That's not possible, when we have already known each other for years now."

"Yes, but from afar."

"It's just like what Madame said -- all of these things, we'll learn about each other overtime, and it will be accepted no matter what. It's all part of the journey. We could sit on that bench over there and spend the next twenty-four hours going over one an-other's life stories. Of course, yours might be a little longer than mine, but..."

"I believe I see what you're saying," he stopped her, "I mean, what's the difference? You tell me about all the people you've known, all the things you've accomplished, and all the challenges you've been through -- it won't make me love you any more or less. I've chosen you, and that's that. There's no backing out now. You couldn't tell me anything right now that would make me walk away. Face it, we are already stuck together."

"Exactly," Fuchsia smirked.

"I just worry... can you say the same? I have been through a lot, although I am not the same person, I'm not so sure you'll accept every little thing about me."

"Of course I will," Fuchsia insisted, "you have to trust me."

"Done," he playfully poked her nose.

"Now, let's rush into this," she grinned, "mermaids and mermen don't really have any laws when it comes to marriage. So let's do this, now. Just us."

"Fuchsia?"

"Yes?"

"Do you take me as your husband, to love me, through death and beyond?"

"I do," she smiled wide, "and do you take me to be your wife, to love me, through death and beyond?"

"I do," he smiled back. "May I kiss you now?"

"Please do!"

The two leaned in for a heartful kiss on the lips. Immediately after, Fuchsia looked up to see a gust of birds flying over them.

The Captain and Fuchsia, husband and wife, the new Father Merman and Mother Mermaid, dove deep into the sea with their green tails guiding them through the depths of the water. Deep down, in the darkest blue, hidden in a crystal cave, they cuddled together and adjusted to a new life.

Things would be much different now. The Captain would no longer sail around on his ship, there was nothing left for him to search for. And Fuchsia would embrace an entirely different life as well.

Fuchsia recalled her younger days as a mermaid -- swimming around, playing and partying with all the other merpeople, and putting on shows for their entertainment. It was a life she had grown bored of -- too comfortable, too easy, no challenges. And then, she embarked upon the ultimate challenge: to live as one with the humans. It was overwhelming, exhausting, and lonely -- but through it all, she learned more about herself in that short timespan than she had ever known her entire life.

The Captain cuddled up with his mermaid, curling his merman tail around her.

"It's still going to take a while to get used to seeing you as a merman," Fuchsia giggled. "You know, C, you said you weren't a true captain, but I completely disagree. You will always be my Captain. And to me, 'C' still stands for 'Captain.'"

The Captain joked to her, "I suppose I can't argue with your flattery."

As the two of them snuggled closer together, there was a sudden shift. Their healing energy had already begun dispersing throughout the water.

"It's happening," Fuchsia said in amazement, wide-eyed, "we're healing the world with our love -- starting with the ocean. And maybe someday -- the entire planet."

"I love you so much," he told her, sleepily.

"I love you more," Fuchsia could barely keep her eyes open, a wave of grogginess thrusted upon her.

And before they could continue speaking, they fell into a deep slumber. Laying together, deep inside their cave, there was now nothing but silence. The two of them had never experienced such a tranquil moment ever before.

At sunrise, Fuchsia felt a twinkling in her lower stomach, and she knew exactly what that meant -- "I'm pregnant!" she announced.

As the days went by, and Fuchsia's belly grew bigger, she had her own crystal ball that she gazed into. Far greater than Madame's handheld crystal, this one was larger than her whole body. Looking into the crystal, she could see and hear those who were praying to her -- to the New Mother Mermaid.

Working together, using their psychic abilities, Fuchsia and her Captain learned how to send wavelengths throughout the water, progressively raising vibrations of the whole sea.

There was a noticeable change among the mermaids and mermen. They were consuming far less sea cocktails. They were engaging in deeper, much more philosophical discussions. And to her surprise, some of them were beginning to genuinely ponder the thought of uniting with the humans.

Fuchsia had hope. For as long as she and the Captain continued to heal their merpeople, someday, their entire species could heal the humans. They could stop them from another inevitable apocalypse. They could live with each other in peace and harmony.

While Mother Mermaid was the sole ruler, after the prior Father Merman had died several hundred years ago, was when morality completely declined among the merpeople. That's when they completely gave up on protecting and helping out the humans -- that's when they turned to drinking, partying, and a life full of mindless play. Mother Mermaid couldn't do it alone -- and if it had been Father Merman, he couldn't have done it alone either.

Fuchsia could see now: that love was the meaning of life. Without love, there is no purpose -- without purpose, there is no hope -- and without hope, there is no healing.

Although his birth name was Cole, and Fuchsia's nickname for him was "C," he would always be her Captain. He was her armor, her protection, her leader. Whenever he lost control of his ship, when his hands would become too shaky to steer the wheel straight, Fuchsia promised to ride out those waves with him. Through the thickest of storms, through bewildering seasickness, she would remain by his side forever.

And for the Captain, Fuchsia would always be his mermaid -- through her enchanting mystery, her fiery passion, and of course, her dazzling charm.

THE END

ABOUT THE AUTHOR

Laura Cyrena Kellogg

Laura Cyrena Kellogg (Lotus Laura) is a blogger for lotuslaura.com, where she writes about mythology, media, spirituality, animals, health, and more -- including occasional short stories -- where the original first draft for "The Captain & the Mermaid" was born. She also conducts psychic readings on crystalauragaze.com

Made in the USA
Middletown, DE
17 July 2021

44339739R00141